LEETCH

Brian Colborne

LEETCH

Contents

For my family.

It's OK to look back but don't stare.
— Alcoholics Anonymous slogan

CHAPTER ONE
It Has To Be Done

Today

Jeff's phone woke him up. It just rang and rang. He rolled over in his bed to turn away from the sun but the damn phone wouldn't stop. He wondered why the machine didn't pick up. He figured the caller would give up in a minute but they didn't. He groaned with displeasure and threw his blankets off. The harsh sun made him squint as he looked around his small bachelor apartment and the phone continued to ring.

"I swear I'm gonna kill whoever that is," he said. He saw the pieces of his answering machine next to the phone. He must have dropped it or smashed it the night before. He picked up the receiver and answered with anger.

"Yeah, what?" he said.

"Oh, hello. Is this Jeff? Jeff Leetch?" the woman said. Jeff didn't recognize the voice.

"Yeah. Who's this?"

"My name is Mary. I'm your mom's neighbour."

"Yeah..."

"I'm so sorry for calling like this. It's just that I've been trying to get a hold of you and, oh, there's no easy way to say it but your mom died last week."

"What?" Jeff said. "Is this some kind of sick prank call? Who is this, really?"

"I'm afraid it's true, dear," Mary said. Jeff poured himself a glass of coke while he listened. "It was liver failure. Believe me, I wish it weren't true." Jeff opened the freezer and topped off his drink with the rest of his vodka. He hadn't even thought about his mom in years and he didn't really know what to say to this woman.

"Are you still there, Jeff?" Mary said.

"Oh yeah, sorry," he said. "So..."

"I wanted to call you because the funeral is tomorrow and I didn't want you to miss it."

"Yeah, of course," Jeff said. "When is it?"

"Noon."

"Well, thanks," he said.

"There's one more thing," Mary said. "You see, it's the house. The landlord said he would clear everything out but I thought you might want to have a look first and collect any personal things you'd like to keep."

"I don't know," Jeff said. He didn't want to go anywhere near that house again.

"She doesn't have anybody else, dear," Mary said. "It has to be done."

"Alright. You said noon, right?"

"Yes. I'll see you there."

"Bye."

Jeff kicked aside the pieces of the broken answering machine and sat in his recliner. He lit a smoke and rubbed the sleep from his eyes. His mouth was as dry as sandpaper and he felt like he was still drunk from the night before. His head hurt from the phone call. The sun and the hangover didn't help. He sipped at his drink and tried to tune everything out. He thought about the night before and started to fill in the blanks.

Last night

Jeff was at The Golden Fleece with his buddy Colin. It was a tiny pub that couldn't hold more than thirty or forty people but it was close to Jeff's place and he liked it. It was owned by an old Irish couple, Sean and Maggie. They knew Jeff well from his frequent visits and always kept an eye on him in case he got too sloppy. Jeff liked the dark wood panel walls and the usual patrons gave it a nice atmosphere. There was the old Scottish lady who came in every night and drank tea while she watched the evening news with the owners. She always said the same things.

"That's just terrible," she said when the news was bad. If a feel-good piece was on, her comment was just as predictable. "Isn't that lovely?" She would look around at everyone for confirmation. There were the hipsters at the dart board who mused about how they always played better with a pint or two in them. Colin fiddled with some wires and lights on the small stage before he went on. He played a set of obscure Brit-rock covers.

"Thank you. I'm Colin Hardcastle," he said as he put his guitar down. Colin was from England but immigrated with his parents when he was young. He was always Jeff's partner in crime whenever they went out. The pub filled up a bit as the night went on. Jeff was at his usual stoop right at the bar and Colin circled in and out to mingle and flirt.

"No, darling. It's Hawdcawstle," Colin said and laid on the accent. Jeff looked over his shoulder and saw that Colin was with a girl who giggled at his pronunciation of any word that contained the letter R. That's when Brody walked in. His name was really Tom Brody but everyone called him by his last name. He was English, too, but he was raised here so he didn't have an accent.

"Oi, Brody. You Northern ninny!" Colin said. Brody spread his lanky arms out.

"You Southern fairy," he said. Colin left his lady friend for a moment to shake hands with his buddy. The girl excused herself and never came back. The two of them joined Jeff at the bar and Brody slapped him on the back.

"What are you filthy motherfuckers saying tonight, huh?" he said. Jeff raised his glass and took a drink.

"Same old," he said. Brody didn't stay put for very long. He never did. He always looked like he had more energy than he knew what to do with. Colin complained about the local rock station. Brody told a dirty story laced with graphic imagery and expletives. The night wore on and Jeff shuffled back to his apartment. The last thing he remembered was the elevator ride.

Today

Jeff butted out his cigarette in the ashtray and let out one last slow exhale of grey smoke. He pulled himself up out of his chair and checked the freezer. There was a little bottle of vodka that had a bit left in it. He opened it and drank what remained in one shot. He eased back down on his recliner and wrestled in his mind whether he would even go to the funeral. *It has to be done*, Mary's voice echoed in his head. He decided to at least head out and brave the sunlight of the late Saturday morning. He stared at the empty bottles scattered around the apartment. Wherever he went, he knew he would need more booze on the way home. He got himself cleaned up and dressed then phoned Colin. He sounded fresh and awake.

"Sure come by, mate," he said. It was a short walk to Colin's house. Jeff stopped at the corner store and bought some cigarettes and a couple of chocolate bars. He left the store and had a smoke while he walked. When he arrived, Colin showed him in and they both lit a cigarette.

"To what do I owe this visit?" Colin said

"I need to borrow a blazer. A black one," Jeff said. They were roughly the same size and Jeff knew Colin wouldn't mind.

"Of course, mate. Why?" Colin said.

"Apparently my mom died." Colin didn't respond. His mouth was open but nothing came out. Jeff knew Colin wouldn't know what to say. He had met his mom a couple times and they knew each other for a long time but it was something they just didn't talk about.

"Jesus..." Colin said. Jeff could tell that Colin was at a loss for his next words so he jumped in.

"Yeah. The funeral is tomorrow so I was hoping I could—"

"Right. Of course. Black? Yeah I have a few," Colin said. He leapt up out of his chair and scurried to his bedroom. He came back with a black blazer and handed it to Jeff.

"Jesus. I'm sorry, Jeff," Colin said.

"Thanks," Jeff said. "Listen. Got anything to drink?"

"Yeah, sure." Colin looked around. "Jack and coke?" Jeff could have cared less what it was. Colin poured them both a glass. He handed one to Jeff and held his own out in front of him.

"To life," Colin said. They clinked their glasses together.

"To life," Jeff said. They sat quietly and enjoyed their drinks. The noise in Jeff's head got further away and he welcomed the silence.

"I should get going," Jeff said as he finished his drink. "I've got a lot to do today."

"Right," Colin said. He gulped down the last of his drink. "If you need anything..." he trailed off.

"Thanks for the blazer, man."

"Anytime, mate," Colin said and showed him out.

Jeff slung the jacket over his shoulder like he saw those guys do in the commercials for the suit store. Then he realized how stupid it was to carry it when he could just wear it so he slipped it on. He walked around downtown for a bit, not really headed anywhere.

He stopped in the park and had a smoke on one of the benches. He thought about the funeral again. He still wasn't sure if he would go. He hadn't spoken to his mom in years and, if he went, that woman would be there. He really didn't want to clear out the house. He started to head back home and passed a bar. He thought about a quick stop for a drink but kept on his way. He thought more as he walked. He wondered who would go to the funeral if he didn't. She had no brothers or sisters. Her parents died a long time ago. Jeff was her only child. His dad sure as hell wouldn't be there. He passed another bar as he walked. He decided to hit the liquor store and stock up for the night. He went in and grabbed two big bottles of vodka. He paid and headed home. As he walked, he didn't think about the funeral. He just clutched his bag with the bottles inside. A smile formed in the corners of his lips. He got home and ordered a large pizza and a big bottle of coke. He figured he could have some in the morning, too, before the funeral.

He had a couple of slices and watched the news on the local channel. He went to the kitchen to grab some more and poured himself a drink while he was up. He grabbed another slice and headed back to his chair. After the news, he watched a movie that Colin loaned to him. He recognized some of the actors from the British movies Colin had shown him and, thanks to his English friends, he understood most of the slang they threw around. It was really just a distraction for Jeff, though. He popped up every now and then to refill his glass. Jeff slipped further and further away. The movie had ended but by then, he didn't even notice.

His alarm woke him up at ten in the morning. He had remembered to set it before he passed out. He was still in his recliner, though. He still had his clothes on, too. His glass was on the table next to him, tipped over. One of the big vodka bottles was in his lap. He must have given up on mixed drinks at some point. He got up and coughed. His stomach felt rotten. He stumbled over to his alarm and turned it off. He tried to ease the storm of acid in his stomach with a slice of leftover pizza. It was a mistake and only made him feel worse. He remembered the antacid in the bathroom.

After he showered and shaved, he felt better. He headed to the closet and chose his garments. It wasn't much of a struggle to decide what to wear since he only had one pair of black pants and one white dress shirt. He had a black tie tucked in the back of his sock drawer. He had to go back to the mirror in the bathroom to get the tie on properly. He looked at himself in the mirror and exhaled. He tried to stop the stream of thoughts that begged him not to go. *It has to be done*, he thought. He gathered his keys and wallet, slipped on the blazer, and fastened the buttons. He had to remind himself to undo the bottom one. He couldn't remember where he had heard that. He took his flask out of the drawer and filled it with vodka. He slipped it in the inside pocket of his jacket.

"Just in case," he said. He decided to take the bus and walk the rest of the way instead of a cab. While he waited for the bus to arrive he smoked two cigarettes and lit one off of the other. After what seemed like a lifetime, the bus turned the corner and hissed as it stopped. The door opened and he and the driver exchanged nods instead of words. The bus was almost empty. He took a seat in the back section. It was a few steps higher than the rest of the bus and he could see everything. As he settled, he felt the flask against his side. *Just in case*, he thought. The bus pulled out and he was on his way.

Jeff rang the bell for his stop and got off the bus. He lit a cigarette right away and started to walk down the road toward the cemetery. He tried to think of who would be there and who he would have to face. He finished his smoke just outside the gates and went in. It wasn't an enormous place so he could easily see where he needed to go across the grounds. He wasn't certain but he didn't see any other services set up. He assumed it was the right one and started toward it with a long exhale.

As he walked, he felt the flask against his side

again. He had done well so far. He wondered how long that would last. He slowed his pace and as he got closer he could make out more details. A woman was already there. Likely his mother's neighbour. *What was her name?* Jeff asked himself. He walked closer and closer. He struggled to remember her name. She hadn't noticed him yet. It finally came to him.

"Mary?" he said. The woman turned around. She looked at him with a furrowed brow. He could tell that she was searching her memory.

"Yes?" she said.

"It's Jeff. Jeff Leetch," he said and stuck out his hand.

"Oh Jeff!" she said. "Sorry." She covered her mouth and lowered her voice. "I didn't recognize you," she said as she shook his hand. "You look so different than your pictures. I wasn't sure if you could make it. It was awfully short notice. How are you holding up, dear?" she said.

"Well..." Jeff started to answer but couldn't think of the right words to say. He wasn't sure how he was holding up.

"Oh I'm sorry, dear," Mary said. "Listen, Jeff, I want you to know that Deb, I mean, your mom, she had everything taken care of for today well in advance. Nothing outstanding." He nodded to show that he knew what she meant.

"OK," Jeff said. He was glad that Mary was the talkative type. It meant he didn't have to navigate the social labyrinth he was faced with at that moment.

"Oh goodness. This can all wait until after," Mary said and motioned for Jeff to have a seat. There were three rows of chairs set up in front of a small hole in the ground. They faced a small raised platform which displayed a wreath of flowers. The stand that held the wreath had a small shelf on it and there was a sash around the wreath itself. Deborah Elizabeth Leetch was written on it. Jeff sat in the middle of the front row. Mary chose the chair on the end to the left of him. They sat in silence and waited for the service to start. Another woman arrived and sat at the right end of the middle row but did not introduce herself. Jeff wondered if she was a coworker or a friend. Maybe she was both. As he looked back, they nodded to greet each other. Shortly after, a man, probably her husband, joined her.

Jeff saw a minister walk toward them. He was followed by a man dressed in a simple black suit. The young one held an urn in one hand a stone plaque in the other. The minister carried a book. It looked like a bible. Mary got up out of her seat to intercept them and Jeff couldn't hear but she pointed over to him. The minister looked in Jeff's direction and motioned for him to come over. Jeff wondered why the minister wanted to talk to him. Mary passed by him as he walked over and she sat back down.

"You are Deborah's son, sir?" the minister said.

"Yes I am," Jeff said.

"Would you like to say a few words?"

"Oh," Jeff said, "I... wouldn't know what to say." The minister closed his eyes and nodded. He had a calm gentleness about him and didn't make Jeff feel bad about it.

"I understand. Let us begin." The minister said and gestured toward the service area. They all walked back and the young assistant handed the urn to the minister. He placed it on the shelf in front of the wreath. The assistant placed the stone next to the small hole. Jeff could see that it was the grave marker. It was simple and factual. Her name was on it along with her date of birth and date of death. The only embellishment was a sparrow on either side of her name. The minister took his place on the raised platform next to the wreath and he was about to begin. Jeff took one last look around. Only four people showed up to his mother's funeral. He drew in a deep breath and exhaled slowly. The minister raised his hands to call attention and everyone straightened up in their seats. He opened his bible and addressed the gathering.

"We are here today to pay our last respects and bid a sad but fond farewell to Deborah Leetch. We are here to also celebrate, honour, and pay tribute to her life and in doing so we express our sincere love and admiration for her. And so this day we've put aside our usual daily activities for a while and gathered to give expression to the thoughts and feelings that well up in us at this time of loss. And because, in one way or another, Deborah's death affects us all. Deborah has gone from us and it is only natural that we should be sad. Though in a practical sense, she's no longer part of our lives and the comfort of having a mother or a friend may indeed be lost, the comfort of having had her in our lives is never lost. To match the grief of losing her, we have the joy of having known her. A joy of which we become especially aware of at this moment as we spend a few minutes in silence and remember Deborah in a time of good health and picture her living image in our minds. We recall the special, personal qualities that made her unique. So we gather to say goodbye and to reflect in a simple, private way on Deborah's life. Let us now spend a few moments in silence and you can each remember Deborah in your own special way."

They all lowered their heads. During the silence, Jeff thought about many things. He wondered why there were only four people there. He remembered her as social and outgoing. She always loved a party. He wondered what must have changed in her later years that so few people would come. He wondered what her days were like. After what felt like forever, the minister raised his head.

"Now we bid a final farewell to our dearly departed Deborah," he said. He moved to the wreath and took the urn in his hands. His assistant joined him and they each held a side by the strings. They knelt on either side of the hole and slowly lowered her remains into the ground. When they finished, the minister stood on his elevated platform and opened his bible again.

"In the midst of life we are in death. Earth to earth. Ashes to ashes. Dust to dust." He made a cross on his chest. "Amen."

"Amen," everyone repeated. The minister closed his bible and approached the mourners to shake their hands and say goodbye. He started with Mary and she thanked him.

"It was my honour," he said and turned to Jeff. *What do I say to him*? Jeff thought to himself. He wiped his palm on the leg of his pants and stood up.

"Thank you for your kind words," Jeff said and shook his hand.

"Of course, my son," the minister said. "Peace be with you." He continued on to the couple behind them and, after an equally short exchange, he and his assistant left, headed toward the main building of cemetery. Mary had the redness in her eyes that people have when they've been crying. He hadn't even noticed during the service.

"It was a lovely service, wasn't it?" she said. Jeff nodded in agreement and she touched his shoulder. "I'm glad you could make it, Jeff." The couple who sat behind him headed to their car. Jeff looked back at the grave. "Would you like some time alone, dear?" Mary said.

"No. Not just yet," he said and checked his watch. "I should head over to the house and get started." Mary looked around the parking area.

"Where is your car?" she said as she reached in her bag. She fished around and pulled her keys out.

"I took the bus," he said.

"Oh. We're going to the same place. Let me drive you?" she said. Jeff felt funny about it but she was right.

"Yeah, thank you," he said. Mary smiled and motioned her head toward a silver car parked in the laneway. They walked over and got in.

"You don't mind if I smoke, do you?" she said as she closed her door and pulled out a long, thin cigarette out of her bag.

"Not at all," Jeff said. He reached inside his coat pocket and pulled out his pack. "May I?" he said as he showed it to her. Mary pulled out an ashtray from the centre console.

"Be my guest," she said. They both lit up their cigarettes and Mary drove off. Jeff gave one look back toward the grave site. The workers were already headed toward the service area with a cart and some shovels to fill in the hole and remove the decorations. Jeff looked out the window as they drove along. It was warm outside and the windows were all the way down. Jeff listened to the sound of the wind and the traffic. After they had finished their cigarettes, they were nearly there. Jeff remembered the area well. Just a few more bends in the road and Mary turned the car on to Wilson Avenue. It was a dead end street and about halfway down the road Mary turned the car into her driveway. Jeff looked out his window at the house next door. It hadn't changed at all. He snapped out of his gaze when he heard Mary roll up her window. He did the same and they both got out.

"Thanks for the ride," he said.

"Of course, dear," she said. "Oh I almost forgot." Mary dug around in her purse and searched for something. She stopped and moved her lips to one side of her face to think. Her eyes widened with recollection and she held her palm up. "Wait here," she said. She went to her front door, unlocked it and stepped inside for a minute. She came back out and proudly held up a keychain.

"Ah," Jeff said. He hadn't thought about that. Mary came over and handed him the keys.

"Wouldn't get too far without these," she

said.

"Yeah," he said and smiled. "Mary, I want to thank you for... well, for everything."

"Think nothing of it, dear," she said and put her hand on his shoulder again. "If you need anything, I'll be home all day. Just knock."

"Thanks again," he said. Mary smiled and turned to go inside. She gave him one last smile before she closed her door. Jeff turned around and looked at the house. He lit another smoke and walked across the lawn to the front walkway. The cement stepping stones were cracked and they crumbled at the sides. He smoked his cigarette and stared at the house. He propped his elbow up with his hand and felt the flask press against his side again. He ran his fingers around its contours and let his mind wander. He finished his cigarette and stepped on the butt. He drew in a large breath and let it heave out of him.

"Here we go..."

CHAPTER TWO
A Thousand Words

Jeff walked up the three concrete steps to the front door. He looked at the keychain in his hand. He didn't know which key would work. He tried one that didn't even go in all the way. The second slid in and he turned the lock open. He put the keys in the side pocket of his blazer and opened the door. As he stepped in and closed the door behind him, he stood in the entryway. There was a small coat closet in front of him and a mirror on the wall to his right. Out of habit he took off his shoes and nudged them into the closet.

He looked around the living room. It was dark inside. The curtains blocked out the sun and the only natural light came from the kitchen window down the hall. Some of the furniture had been replaced but it looked like it always did in there. The TV was pointed straight at the couch. There were two small end tables and a long coffee table with a big glass ashtray in the middle. The beige carpet was darkened by a few cigarette burns. His mom used to fall asleep on the couch with a cigarette. There was an old recliner next to the couch that helped divide the living room from the small dining area. Jeff looked down the hallway. It ran right down the middle of the house. On the left there was the bathroom and his old bedroom. To the right was the side entrance, the kitchen, his mother's room, and the stairs that led down to the basement. Jeff walked down the hall and peered into each room. He returned to the living room and turned around slowly. He scratched the top of his head as he looked around. He had no idea where to start. He turned on the floor lamp in the corner and sat on the couch. He pulled out his cigarettes and lit one. He stood back up and paced around the coffee table. Reality started to sink in and he reached into the inside pocket of his jacket. He twisted the top of the flask back and forth in his fingers.

He went back into the kitchen and opened the fridge to look inside. There wasn't much in there so he looked in the freezer. *Holy shit*, he thought. There were three large vodka bottles, all full. They stood lined up like soldiers awaiting their orders. There was another open bottle that was nearly empty. Jeff grabbed it and looked for a glass in the cupboard. He poured out the rest of the bottle and looked in the pantry cupboard. He found a bottle of coke and topped off his glass. He took a slow sip and was more relaxed so he decided to start in his old room.

He walked in and sat down on the bed. It was made up to be a guest room but the bed was the same one from when he was young. He took another mouthful of his drink and remembered how his bedroom looked back then. It wasn't much different but there were no toys or clothes scattered on the floor. There were no posters on the wall. There was no stereo with a tape of songs he had recorded from the radio. There was just the bed against the wall, a dresser and a night stand with a lamp on it. He put his drink down on the small stand next to the bed and got up to look in the dresser. He opened the top drawer and found nothing but a bible. It was like one of those ones they leave in hotel rooms. He thought it was strange. His mom never showed any interest in religion. He was surprised there was even a minister at her funeral. The second drawer just had some blankets and sheets. The bottom drawer was full of framed photos. On top was a picture of his mom and dad that was taken before Jeff was born. He had seen it before but his mom had taken it down when Jeff was little. He took all the pictures and laid them out on the bed. He picked up his drink and surveyed them like someone admiring a painting in an art gallery.

There were a few of his grandparents and some of just his mom but it was mostly pictures of his mom and dad. They looked really happy. They were partying, laughing, and kissing. His mom was big on pictures. She always bought those disposable cameras and would fill photo albums with the prints.

If there were nice ones, she would make enlargements and buy frames to hang them in the hallway or her room. There were a lot of them still hung up but for some reason, these ones were tucked away. Stuffed in a drawer in an unused room. The last time he was there they were still up on the wall but that was a long time ago. He wondered what prompted their removal.

Jeff focused on the only professional photo of the bunch. It was a family portrait from one of those department store photo studios. He picked it up and gulped some more of his drink. There was the whole gang, posed and smiling.

29 years ago

"Hurry up, Jeff!" Deb called out from the bathroom. Jeff was in his room, looking at the horrible sweater his mom had laid out for him. It was the same one he had to wear for picture day at school. It was blue wool and had a big, black stripe across the chest.

"OK, mom!" he yelled back. He put it on over his t-shirt and ran out to put on his dress shoes. He wondered why he had to wear his nice shoes when they weren't even going to be in the picture. He zoomed past his dad who was watching wrestling on TV and finishing a beer.

"Jimmy! Are you ready?" Deb said.

"Yeah, yeah," Jimmy said and turned off the TV. He got up with a grunt and crunched the empty can in his hand. He took it to the garbage can in the kitchen and let out a loud belch. Jeff was waiting at the front door when his mom finally emerged from the bathroom. She was wearing the same blue and purple flowered dress she always wore for a special occasion. She looked at Jimmy in his orange plaid shirt and brown corduroys.

"Ready?" she said and looked him up and down.

"All dressed up. What do you think, Deb?" he said and turned around with his arms out. She looked at him and smirked.

"Well," she said, "it's not jeans and a t-shirt." She looked back at Jeff. "Let's go." Jeff made a whooping noise as he barreled out the front door and down the steps. They all got in the car and drove off to the mall. It was nice out that day. The sun was warm but a cool breeze cut through it. The windows were down because his parents were smoking so Jeff enjoyed it even more. When they arrived, Jimmy parked the car in front of the department store entrance.

"OK, let's get this over with," he said and shut off the engine. Deb looked at him with a pleading glance. Jeff could tell that she was excited about the portrait and it upset her that Jimmy was treating it like a chore that was keeping from his weekend. As they got out, Jimmy pulled a flask from his back pocket and took a swig.

"Ahh," he said. Deb took Jeff by the hand and they walked toward the entrance. Jimmy locked the car and followed them. They went into the photo studio and Deb checked in with the man at the desk.

"Right this way, Mrs. Leetch," he said and showed them the way in. "My name is Gerry. It's nice to meet you folks." He looked up at Jimmy and held out his hand.

"Jimmy Leetch," he said and gave him a single shake. Gerry looked down at Jeff and bent down with his hands on his knees.

"And what might your name be, big fella?" he said.

"I'm Jeff."

"And how old are you?"

"I'm five," Jeff said as he held out his hand to show his age. Gerry took the opportunity to high five him.

"Great," he said. "Wanna take some pictures?"

"OK," Jeff said and they gathered in the posing area. After they had taken a few shots, Gerry showed Jeff's parents the options they had for print packages and showed them some sample shots. Jeff was colouring at the kids table and noticed his mom and dad arguing over money. Gerry excused himself to give them a minute to decide. Jimmy took the flask out of his pocket again and drank a big gulp. They argued some more and his mom gave in to Jimmy's side of it.

Gerry came back a moment later and he settled the bill with Jimmy. Gerry told them he would call the prints came in.

"Bye, guys!" Gerry said. They all bid him farewell and Jeff gave him a wave as they left. Jimmy walked quickly out the doors and toward the car. Jeff struggled to keep the pace with his mom. Jimmy unlocked the car and looked around the lot before he took another drink from his flask. He waited for them to get buckled in and sped away.

Jeff could tell he was mad about something but he didn't know what it was. On the way home, his parents were quiet while they smoked their cigarettes. Deb butted hers out and spoke.

"Jimmy, I was—" she was interrupted by a hard slap across the face that startled Jeff.

"You don't tell people we can't afford something!" Jimmy said. "You trying to make me look like a chump?" Deb shook her head no as she cried and held her face. Jimmy kept going.

"That nimrod photographer thinks we can't afford a few damn pictures. We can afford what I say we can afford!"

"Sorry, Jimmy," Deb whispered and put her head down. She was still holding her face. Jeff knew not to say anything unless he was spoken to so he sat quietly for the rest of the ride.

When they got home his mom helped him out of the car and he saw a red handprint on her cheek. When they went in, his dad went straight to the fridge and cracked open another can of beer before he flopped down the couch to channel surf. Jeff's mom told him to get changed out of his nice clothes and play in his room. His room looked right into the kitchen and he could see his mom smoking a cigarette at the little table.

After she finished, she made him a snack and told him to come eat at the table. Deb went back to the kitchen while Jeff ate. She came back out with a beer and brought to his dad.

"Jimmy?" she said. He looked up at her and

she held the can out as a peace offering. He accepted and took it from her. She sat next to him on the couch and looked right at him. "Thanks for the pictures," she said. Jimmy looked back at her but he still had a scowl on his face. She lowered her head. After a second he put his hand on her thigh and smiled.

"Well," he said, "I know you like that stuff." He put his finger under her chin and lifted her head back up. They looked at each other and Jimmy gave her a kiss.

A few days later they got a call from the photography studio. Deb picked up the prints and bought a frame for the big one. She mailed some smaller ones to her friends and replaced the old photo in her wallet with a new one. She kept a few for her albums as well. Jeff could tell that she liked them. She hung the big picture on the wall in the hallway and stood back to admire it.

"A nice family portrait," she said to Jeff. He looked up at her and nodded in approval.

Today

Jeff put the pictures back in the dresser drawer. He kept the portrait aside and thought he might keep it. He didn't have any pictures of his family at his place. He closed the drawer and tucked the picture under his arm. He grabbed his glass from the night table. He had finished his drink and he was about to go get a refill. He stopped mid-step and tossed the picture back on the bed. *Nice portrait?* he thought. *Yes. Nice family? No.*

CHAPTER THREE
Life Imitates Art

Jeff closed the door behind him and went to the kitchen. He cracked open another bottle of vodka and poured himself a glass. He decided to check out the basement. As he went down the stairs, he banged his head where the ceiling started. He remembered his dad doing that all the time. Jeff yelled out some curse words to alleviate the pain. He rubbed his head a bit and turned on the light. It was cooler down there and it felt nice. He looked around the unfinished open space. The washer and dryer were in the far back corner. There were shelves of magazines and old books. Piled up along the wall were boxes of Christmas decorations and linens. The furnace was smack in the middle of everything. Almost buried under old boxes was his moms filing cabinet.

He set his drink on top and opened the top drawer. She kept everything in there. Tax records, school photos, receipts, and anything remotely official was in there. Jeff thumbed through some things and came across a report card from when he was in the first grade. It was in an envelope that had a spot underneath the school information where Jeff had to draw a picture for Thanksgiving. He opened the envelope and pulled out the papers. It had all his tests and reports from the first part of the school year.

On top of the stack was the class picture. Jeff chuckled at how he looked in the photo. He had a big goofy smile and looked happy back then. He was in the front row and he had a big grass stain on the knee of his pants. He kept looking and found an early report from parent/teacher night.

28 years ago

It was late September and the days were warm but it got cooler in the evening. Jimmy put on his jean jacket while Jeff got ready to go. The school wasn't far from their house so they decided to walk. Jeff saw his dad slip a silver flask in his back pocket. Deb put on a light coat and told Jeff to put one on, too.

He grabbed his neon blue and yellow windbreaker. It made so much noise and Jimmy shook his head at the sound it made when Jeff put it on. Jimmy and Deb walked side by side and smoked while Jeff whooshed back and forth in front of them.

"Why are we going to school at night, mom?" he said. He walked backwards and waited for her answer.

"So we can meet your teacher," she said. Jeff accepted the answer and just carried on, whooshing down the sidewalk in his noisy windbreaker. Jimmy chuckled at Jeff's antics as he drank from his flask. Once they arrived, there were signs telling parents where to go but Jeff took the lead.

"Mom, this way!" he said. "Dad, follow me!"

"Mmm hmm," Jimmy said. They followed Jeff to his classroom. He showed them his desk and where he hung his coat. He was very excited to show off his little world. Once everyone had arrived, the teacher, Mrs. Pryce, had each family gather around the desk of their child. She talked about the daily routines and the curriculum. Jimmy made a joke that Jeff didn't really get but Deb slapped Jimmy's arm to tell him to stop. Jimmy was the only one who laughed. Mrs. Pryce gave a little tour of the classroom and invited everyone to the gym so the kids could play while the parents talked with the teacher.

Jeff was playing tag with his friends when Jimmy yelled over to him.

"Jeff!" he said. "Let's go. Now." Jeff knew by the tone of voice that his dad meant business. Jeff hurried over and they left. As soon as they were through the doors, Jimmy took a big drink from his flask. Jeff knew that his dad was mad about something but didn't know what. Nobody spoke the whole way home. The only sound was Jeff's noisy windbreaker. When they got home, Jimmy went straight to the fridge for a beer then sat in his spot on the couch. Jeff knew not to bother him when he was mad. Deb ushered Jeff to his room.

"Play with your toys, sweetie," she said. "Then it'll be bedtime soon." Jeff played with his rubber wrestling figures. He heard his parents talking about him while he played. Mrs. Pryce wanted to see them again to discuss Jeff's behaviour further. Jimmy was mad because he had to waste another night at the school.

"How the hell bad could it be?" he said. "Numbskulls."

"We'll have to see," Deb said. Jimmy had finished his beer and pointed at Jeff on his way to the kitchen.

"You best not be gettin' in any trouble, boy-o," he said. Jeff gave him a puzzled look and Jimmy just rolled his eyes and continued on. Deb came in and told Jeff to get ready for bed.

He put on his pyjamas and housecoat and did his nightly routine before he went to bed.

A few days went by and once more they were off to school in the evening. They went right to Jeff's classroom and Mrs. Pryce was waiting with the principal. He greeted them when they came in.

"Mr. And Mrs. Leetch. Thanks for coming," he said. " Hi, Jeff."

"Hey, Mr. R," Jeff said. The principal had a long Italian name that none of the kids could pronounce so everyone called him Mr. R. Jeff's teacher had some activities for him to do while they spoke with his parents at her desk. They talked in low voices but Jeff could see that they were showing something to his mom and dad. Deb kept looking back at him with a strange look on her face. They talked for a long time while Jeff coloured some pictures and read some story books. When they finished, Jimmy got up and stomped out.

"Let's go," he said as he passed by. Deb grabbed Jeff by the hand and led him out. Jimmy was mad so Jeff knew not to rile him up by asking what happened. When they got home, Deb pulled a piece of paper out of her purse. Jimmy snatched it away from her and shook it front of Jeff's face.

"What the hell is this, Jeff?" he said. Jeff looked at the paper. It was a picture he drew in class.

"Teacher said we had to draw a picture of our whole family," he said. The picture was a pencil crayon drawing that showed Jeff playing with a soccer ball and his parents off to the side. The top of the picture said mom, dad, and me. Jimmy was holding a can in one hand and there were motion lines to show that he was hitting Deb with the other. She had big blue tears in the picture.

"So you drew this?" Jimmy said. He was fuming. His lips curled down under his moustache and his nostrils flared. Deb bent down to Jeff's level and cut in.

"Jeff, why did you draw us like this?" she said. Jeff looked back and forth at his parents and the drawing. He shrugged his shoulders. His voice felt trapped. He knew he was in trouble but couldn't understand why. He did what his teacher asked. Jimmy breathed angry breath down to Jeff's face. His eyes blurred with tears. He was confused but he knew that the picture made his dad angry.

"I'm sorry, dad," he said. It was all that he could get out before he started to cry. Jimmy didn't seem to like the answer. He grabbed Jeff by the arm and pulled him so quickly that it felt like he was being dragged by a car. Jimmy stormed down the hall and Jeff's feet barely touched the floor along the way. Jimmy opened

Jeff's room and shoved him on the bed. His head hit the wall on the way down. He raised his arm to rub the sore spot but winced because his shoulder felt like it was on fire. Jimmy pointed down at him from the doorway.

"You stay in there and think about you've done," he said. "And keep quiet." Jeff nodded as tears ran down his cheeks. He laid down on his bed and rubbed his shoulder. He listened to his parents argue for a long time. Jimmy was shouting.

"He made me look like an asshole, Deb!" he said. "Like some kind of white trash drunk."

"They're just worried about Jeff," Deb said.

"Pfft. Yeah they should worry about him," Jimmy said. "That kid is messed up."

"They said they're worried because kids act out what they see at home. They don't want him to hit people, too," Deb said.

"What did you say?" Jimmy said. Deb didn't answer. "What the hell did you just say?" he pressed again. Deb stayed silent. Then Jeff heard a bunch of glass break and fall to the floor. Jeff sat up on his bed. He could see his mom in the kitchen. There was a puddle of brown liquid on the floor around her feet.

"What did you say?" Jimmy asked again. Deb stood silent. She stood there with pride and defiance. Jeff never saw his mom look at Jimmy that way. She stood up to him like he was a schoolyard bully.

"They don't want him to be like you!" she said. Jeff couldn't see his dad clearly but he did see the back of his hand come down across his mom's face. There was a loud crack of skin colliding together and Deb screamed as she fell to the floor. She laid there in the puddle of brown liquid, surrounded by the broken glass and holding her face. Jimmy stepped over her and stopped when he saw Jeff through the door. They stared at each other but neither one of them said a word. Jeff never saw his dad so infuriated. There was so much rage in his eyes. He looked like a different person. The light cast shadows on his face that only intensified his frightening glare. The only sound was the short, intense breath shooting from his nostrils. Jeff had no idea what his dad was going to do next and he just stared right back at him. He thought they would be locked in this stalemate forever when Jimmy turned and went down the hallway. Jeff heard the front door slam and the car screeched away. He got up from his bed and went to the kitchen but his mom held up her hand to stop him.

"Stay back, Jeff. There's glass in here," she said. Jeff stood in the entryway while his mom picked herself up off the floor. She cleaned up the glass pieces and mopped the floor. She cried and sniffled the whole time. When she had finished, she came over to Jeff and bent down to look him in the eyes.

"Are you OK?" she said. Jeff saw the huge red mark on the side of her face and he nodded without saying anything. His shoulder still hurt but at that moment he didn't care. Deb gave him a hug and told him to get ready for bed. Jeff turned to go back to his room and saw the picture he drew crumpled up on the floor.

When Jeff woke up in the morning, his dad wasn't there. His head had a sore bump on it but it wasn't that bad. His forearm had a red mark on it in the shape of his dad's hand.

Eventually, it bruised and Jeff wore long sleeve shirts to school to cover it. His shoulder got better, too. His mom's face seemed fine but Jeff could tell that she used her makeup to help hide the bruise.

One day when Jeff came home from school, his mom was having a nap on the couch. He took his jacket off and put it in the closet. It seemed emptier than usual. He went to the bathroom and noticed that all of his dad's shaving stuff was gone.

He went to the kitchen to get some juice. There was always beer in the fridge but not now. Deb stirred awake and joined Jeff in the kitchen. She stroked his head and poured some juice for the both of them. She took the glasses out to the dining room and they sat down at opposite ends of the table.

"Is dad coming back?" Jeff said. He looked at his mom as she drew in a big breath and let it out. She looked back at him and told him the truth.

"No, Jeff. He's not," she said. Jeff looked at her and didn't speak. "Want to talk about it?" she said. He shook his head no and touched his forearm. The bruise was still sore. He thought about his dad standing over his mom and the look in his eyes that night. It was the last time he ever saw him.

CHAPTER FOUR
You Never Forget Your First

Today

Jeff put the school stuff back in the filing cabinet. He looked through some other files and stopped on one with some receipts in it. There was one from the hospital. It was a medical bill with Jeff's name on it.

17 years ago

Jeff got invited to a house party at Lori's house. Well, every student at Armstrong High did. Her parents were out of town and word got out pretty fast. Saturday night was going to be the first big party of the year. Someone knew a guy who knew a guy, or something like that, was getting the booze and it was shaping up to be quite a shindig. Jeff wasn't just excited about the party. He thought Lori was great and this was his chance to get to know her better. When the night came, he got dressed in his best digs. He called Colin and Brody to confirm their plans. They met at Jeff's' place and walked from there.

"I hope they've got good tunes," Colin said.

"It's gonna be fuckin' wicked," Brody said. Jeff wasn't so sure. He wasn't against having a drink or two but getting wasted didn't look like so much fun to him. He was going for Lori. His nerves were shot by the time they got there. They timed it so they would arrive, as Colin said, fashionably late.

They were greeted at the door by a guy from their gym class, Scott, who recognized them and showed them in. Jeff was hit with the smell of cigarettes and pot. That new band from Orange County blasted from the stereo. The house was full of people from school and some others that Jeff didn't recognize. Scott pointed up to the bathroom at the top of the stairs.

"Beers are in there," he said. They went up and saw the tub, full of ice, and the necks of the brown bottles poked out.

"Nice," Colin said and grabbed one for each of them. They opened them and Jeff took his first sip. Beer didn't taste the way he thought it would. For some reason he always thought it would be like root beer but maybe a little better.

After that first mouthful he didn't understand what all the fuss was about. They went back downstairs to mingle. Jeff lit a cigarette and joined the smokers who were huddled around a big glass ashtray in the living room. Colin and Brody inspected the music selection next to the stereo. Jeff finished his smoke and wandered to the kitchen. Lori was there mixing vodka drinks and laughing with her friends. The counter was covered with liquor bottles of all shapes and sizes. Some pop song came on and Lori's group squealed in delight before they took off to dance. Jeff drank his beer slowly with Scott and some other guys in the kitchen. He felt a little out of place with new people. Scott poured some vodka in a red party cup and splashed some cola in it. He handed it to Jeff.

"Here, man. Try this," he said. Jeff thanked him and took a big gulp. It hurt his throat and burned all the way down. Once he had swallowed it all, he coughed like he was choking. The guys around him chuckled.

"Good shit, isn't it?" one of them said. Jeff's stomach felt strange but good.

"Not bad, I guess," he said.

"This kind is the best," Scott said. "You don't even smell like booze when you drink it." Jeff smiled and raised his cup to his new companions. He left to find his friends.

As he roamed the house he alternated

between his party cup in one hand and the beer bottle in the other. The beer started to taste better but the warm tingle of the vodka was wonderful. It spread out from his chest to his limbs and then his fingers and toes. He ended up circling back to the kitchen.

Scott and the others were gone and had been replaced by a group of jocks who were arguing about the merits of some football player. Jeff turned his focus to the bottle of clear liquid on the counter. He filled his glass and added some more coke before he wandered back out. He still didn't see his friends so he went upstairs. The bathtub full of brown bottles reminded him that he was nearly done his beer. He took one last chug and grabbed a fresh one. He decided to check the rooms for Colin and Brody. The first door was locked but the second one was ajar so he nudged it open.

"Anybody home?" he said as he barged in. A girl's voice came from the bed.

"What the hell?" It was Lori. She was with an older guy that Jeff didn't recognize. "Get lost, perv!" Jeff almost fell backwards as he tried to retreat. The guy laughed at Jeff and told him to shut the door on his way out.

"Yeah, sure. Sorry," Jeff said. He pulled the door closed just as Colin and Brody came out of the room at the end of the hall. They were followed by a cloud of smoke and the reek of weed.

"Oi, Jeff!" Colin said as he laughed and coughed. "Why the red face?"

"Huh?"

"You're all red, mate."

"I am?"

"What's in there?" Colin said. Jeff turned to make sure that the door was closed.

"Nothing." They all heard a moan from inside the room. Brody's face twisted to a sinister grin.

"Oh, Jeffy," he said, "did you see naked hugging?" They all laughed and Brody knocked on the door.

"Go away!" the guy said. They heard the lock and Brody yelled at the door.

"Don't break the bed, lovebirds!" He made moaning sounds of his own. There was a loud thud on the door and the three of them scurried away, giggling. When they were safely back downstairs, they headed outside for some fresh air. Colin and Jeff smoked while Brody complained about the cold. Jeff offered him his drink.

"This will warm you up," he said.

"What is it?"

"Vodka and coke," Jeff said. Brody waved it away.

"Nah, I'll stick to beer." Jeff shrugged his shoulders and drank some more. Each mouthful tasted less offensive and made him feel warmer inside. He finished his drink and brought his friends with him to the kitchen to make another. As he drank it down, Colin looked at Jeff with concern.

"Mate, she's just a bird," he said. "Don't take it too hard."

"What do you mean?" Jeff said as he swallowed.

"Lori," Colin said and pointed his eyes to the ceiling.

"Oh," Jeff said. "Yeah. No big deal, man." He chugged down his drink and made another. He abandoned his half empty bottle of beer and they went back outside to smoke. As they finished, a fight spilled out of the front door and a circle formed in the front yard. Jeff couldn't tell what it was all about but it fizzled as quickly as it started and never amounted to more than a few shoves. Most of the crowd went back in and Jeff followed.

He stayed in the kitchen and thought about what Colin had said earlier. Jeff should have felt upset. Lori was with some loser in a backwards hat and he didn't even get a chance to talk to her. The girl he had spent countless days thinking about, countless nights dreaming about, was alone in a room with a backwards hat guy. He should have felt something. Instead, all he felt was the warmth in his chest and the numbness of his lips and fingers. Instead, he felt every care in the world melt away. Each refill of the red party cup made him feel better and better. He finished one after another and went outside again.

There was still a bit of a crowd hanging around, buzzing about the brawl that never was. Jeff walked further away to find his friends. When he didn't see them, he thought they might have gone down the street. He didn't see them down there, either. He figured they must have headed home and forgot to tell him. That sort of thing happened at parties, he supposed. Before he knew it he was almost home and his cup was empty. He tossed it on the ground and lit a cigarette. He stood in front of the art museum and stared at a big metal rhinoceros.

The flood lights reflected off of its side and he wondered why they chose a giant metal beast to be featured on display. Why a rhino, of all things? There were no rhinos around. Why that piece of art over any others? Why not some abstract sculpture that embodied some abstract emotion? Why, why, why?

He realized that he had finished his smoke and went to light another but his eyes were heavy. Despite the light of the shimmering rhinoceros, darkness crept in around his field of vision. His legs felt like toothpicks, unable to hold his body upright. The last thing he remembered was cold grass on his cheek and someone calling his name. The mighty silver rhino was swallowed by blackness.

* * *

When he woke, Jeff was greeted by the face of his mother. She looked sad, happy and angry all within a few seconds.

"Oh thank God," she said. Jeff rubbed his eyes but didn't speak. He felt exhausted and wasn't sure where he was. He was about to ask when Deb spoke again.

"Well, Jeff," she said, "you've certainly done it this time." Jeff was confused.

"What happened?" he said and looked around the room. He was in a hospital. There were rows and rows of beds separated by curtains. His mom breathed out through her nose.

"Brody and Colin said you passed out on the way home and they found you," she said. Jeff scrambled to think of a plausible excuse but he didn't know what his friends had told her.

"Yeah, umm, I wasn't feeling so—"

"Save it, Jeff." Deb held her hand up and interrupted. "I know everything." She didn't yell at him and that scared Jeff. He expected her to lose it on him but she just recounted what happened in a very matter-of-fact way. He was treated for alcohol poisoning and they kept him overnight as a precaution. Eventually they discharged him and they were both silent on the ride home. When they got in, Jeff made himself a sandwich. He saw his mom sitting on the couch and smoking. She wasn't watching TV or talking on the phone. She just sat there. Jeff went to his room and dozed off. He woke up in the late afternoon. The sound of music had stirred him from his sleep. His mom was listening to the classic rock station on the radio. The song finished by the time Jeff walked out of his room. Deb was in the kitchen making meatloaf when she noticed him.

"There you are," she said. "Sit down. Let's talk." Jeff sat at the small kitchen table. He figured he would be grounded for life after this one. She had never stayed calm when he got caught for something before. She was usually predictable. She would scream, interrogate, scream again, and dole out punishment. This was different, though. Jeff saw a vodka bottle on the counter. She didn't drink like his dad did but there was always vodka in the freezer.

"So what do you have to say for yourself?" she said. Jeff opened his mouth but when he looked her in the eye he couldn't think of a single word. Deb shook her head and sat at the table.

"Seventeen years old," she said. "Seventeen years old and in the hospital for alcohol poisoning. What were you thinking, Jeff?" He struggled to come up with something more meaningful than shrugged shoulders.

"I didn't mean to," he said.

"You didn't mean to pass out drunk on the side of the road?"

"No."

"What about underage drinking? Didn't mean to?"

"Umm."

"And lying about where you were going? Didn't mean to, right?" Deb looked him straight in the eyes and he lowered his head. It wasn't from shame, though. He got caught and felt stupid for going one step over the line. If he didn't have that last drink he might have made it all the way home. He could have pretended to feel sick. Maybe she wouldn't have bought it but at least it would have been believable. He wouldn't make that mistake next time. He knew right then that there would indeed be a next time. It was only a matter of how long he had to wait for it. How many days? How many hours until the world would tingle away and the warmth would radiate through his body again? His mother's voice snapped him out of his daydream.

"You could have died, Jeff," she said. "I want you to promise me you'll never do that again." Jeff looked up and nodded. He wouldn't do that again. He would stay in control. He would make sure that no one even knew.

"OK, mom."

"Good," she said. "I don't want you ending up like your father." Her words filled him with rage and he shot up from his chair.

"What did you say?"

"Your father," Deb said. "He let it control his life. And ours." Jeff slammed his fist on the table.

"I'm nothing like him!"

Jeff, I was only—"

"What about you, mom?" he said and pointed to the bottle on the counter. "Some role model you are."

"How dare you!" Deb said as she rose from her chair. She slapped Jeff hard across the face and her long nails raked his cheek. His lip was cut by his teeth and he felt blood trickle down his chin.

"You bitch!" he said and wiped his mouth. He glanced at the blood on the back of his hand and was struck on his nose. This time it wasn't a slap, it was a fist. Deb had knocked him off balance and he stood hunched over, holding his face. Blood ran from his nose and pooled on the tile floor. Jeff looked up at her as he tried to stop the bleeding.

"Are you done?" he said. Deb lowered her hand but the anger in her face didn't subside.

"You're just like him," she said through her

teeth. She stormed out through the front door. Jeff cleaned himself up in the bathroom and took the meatloaf out of the oven when the timer rang. He mopped up the bloody mess on the floor and made himself a plate for dinner. He watched some TV for a couple of hours before his mom came back home. She stopped in the entryway and they both looked at each other. Jeff could tell by her red eyes and matted eyelashes that she had been crying. Jeff took his plate to the kitchen. He went to his room and closed the door behind him. They didn't speak to each other that night.

Jeff woke to an empty house. He got a bowl of cereal and sat down on the couch. A note was on the coffee table. Jeff set down his bowl and read it.

Grounded 1 month
Mom

Jeff finished eating and cleared the table. He crumpled the note and tossed it in the garbage. His mom came home after work and asked if he got her note.

"Yep," he said. Deb didn't say anything. After that, things were different between them. Usually, no more than a few syllables were exchanged at a time.

The month of punishment passed and Jeff

decided to find an after school job. He filled out an application at the fast food place closest to his house and they hired him a few days later.

He worked as much as they would let him. It wasn't just to avoid being at home but so he was able to pay for his own liquor. He didn't want to wait for the next big party. He was able to get it easily enough. He started out by getting college students to buy it for him but that always came with the promise of buying them something for the trouble. There was also the risk of being ripped off.

"What are ya gonna do about it?" the older kids would say. He asked around and got himself a fake ID. It wasn't anything fancy but it was good enough. After a few visits to the same store he was able to get away without being asked to see it every time. He started out only drinking on the weekends when his mom would go out with her friends. Every now and then, Colin and Brody would come over. Then Deb started working a second job that kept her out later during the week and Jeff found himself alone and bored. Soon, weekends turned to every few days. By his senior year it was every day. At school he filled his water bottle with vodka and sipped it throughout the day. His grades slipped but he didn't care much about that. He was never in the running for valedictorian to begin with. Nothing bothered

Jeff much, as long as he quenched his thirst.

It wasn't long after Jeff graduated that he found an apartment of his own. He hardly ever spoke to his mom by then. On the day he moved out, Brody came by with his pickup and they loaded Jeff's things while Deb was at work. Before he left, he wrote a note and left it on the coffee table.

Moved out.
Jeff

He didn't leave his address or phone number. Every now and then she tried to get a hold of him but Jeff wasn't able to let the past go. As far as he was concerned, she drew first blood.

CHAPTER FIVE
The House Of Red And Gold

Today

Jeff went upstairs and opened the door to his mother's room. It was the same as always except for a few knick-knacks that were replaced and there were less photos on the wall. They were taken down and put in the drawer in his old room. He went over to the closet. It was one of those doors that slid open side to side. Jeff opened the left side. It had winter coats and some dresses in it. The top shelf was full of blankets and sheets. Jeff opened the other side and found some shoes on the floor and more clothes hanging up. It was mostly sweats and kick around clothes. At the end of the row he saw a red hockey jersey. He took it off the hanger and held it out in front of him. The front had TITANS written in yellow above a bearded face with lighting for hair. They were the minor league hockey team in town and Jeff used to love them. His dad loved them, too. They would watch them on the local station every Friday night when he was young. As he got older he stopped following hockey so closely but he always remained a Titans fan. He even had an old t-shirt at home from one of the games he went to.

5 years ago

Jeff was calling to try to win free tickets to the game when the DJ at the radio station answered.

"Congratulations, you are caller 96," she said. "What's your name?"

"Hey, it's Jeff," he said. He was excited. He had never gotten through before and he was certain he had the winning answer.

"Jeff, do you know the rules?"

"You bet."

"Then let's play," she said. The game was to guess what the noise was from a sound clip. The sound played after a countdown.

"What is your guess, Jeff?"

"Is it a typewriter?" He waited for a response from the DJ. Some victorious music played.

"Jeff, you have won yourself two tickets to the

Titans game tomorrow night," she said. They stayed on the phone and she gave him instructions to pick them up. He stopped by on his way to work that day and left with his prize. He had two tickets but nobody to go with. Any of his friends would like to go with him but he had another idea.

When he got to the restaurant, he checked the schedule to see if Ashley was working that night. She was a waitress and Jeff knew that she liked the Titans because she sometimes wore a shirt with their logo on it when she left work. He also knew that she didn't have a boyfriend so he thought this was his chance to ask her out. A couple of hours into his shift, he spotted his opportunity. Ashley went out the back door for a cigarette and Jeff grabbed a bag of garbage. He told the other kitchen guys that he would be right back. He tossed the bag in the dumpster and turned around to face Ashley. She smiled and greeted him.

"Hey, Jeff," she said.

"Oh hey, Ash," he said and started to go back inside. He stopped as he reached for the door. "Maybe I'll join you." He took out a cigarette and lit it. "Big plans for the weekend?"

"Nothing much," she said.

"Working tomorrow?" He knew very well she wasn't and she shook her head no.

"How about you?" she said.

"Well I just won these tickets on the radio," he said. He took them out of his back pocket and showed them to her. "Wanna go with me?" Ashley looked up from the tickets and smiled.

"Absolutely!" she said. Jeff smiled back. They both lived fairly close to the arena so they agreed to meet at the gate. Jeff spent the rest of the day smiling and whistling a happy tune.

When he got home he ordered a pizza and watched some movies. He also celebrated his good fortune with some drinks.

The next thing he knew it was morning and he was laying sideways in his bed. He still had his clothes on from the day before. He sat up and looked at his watch. It was almost noon. He got himself together and phoned Colin to see what he was up to.

"Not much," Colin said. "Still want to meet The Ale House later?"

"What are you talking about?" Jeff said.

"You called me last night, mate."

"Really? Oh... yeah," Jeff said. He had no idea what Colin was talking about. "Meet me on the patio, though. Four-ish?"

"Right," Colin said. "Ta."

Jeff got to the bar right on time. It was adjacent to the arena and Jeff would be able to see the entry gates from the patio. Colin was already there with a pitcher of beer and two glasses on the table.

"Oi, oi," Colin said. Jeff joined him and positioned his chair so he could keep an eye out for Ashley. Colin poured them both a glass and held his up.

"Cheers," Jeff said and they clinked their glasses together.

"So tell me about this bird of yours, mate," Colin said.

"Ashley? She's a waitress at work. She's pretty cool," Jeff said. They drank and chatted and ordered more beer. Just before 6:30 Jeff saw Ashley walking down the street. Colin was playing a set at The Golden Fleece that night and invited Jeff to bring Ashley by after the game. Jeff settled his tab at the bar and grabbed some cash from the machine on his way out. He walked across the street to meet Ashley. She was wearing her Titans shirt under a leather jacket. Jeff thought she looked fantastic. Much better than in those ugly uniforms the wait staff had to wear at work. She waved to him.

"Hi, Jeff," she said. He waved back then pointed to the lineup forming at the entrance of the arena.

"Ready, Ash?"

"Oh yeah," she said. "I can't believe you won tickets. I just love the playoffs. Don't you?"

"It's pretty awesome," he said.

They went in and saw a huge banner in the lobby that read *The House of Red and Gold.* The building buzzed and pulsated with excitement. If the Titans beat the Bulls, they would move on to the finals.

Everyone was given little red towels on the way in. It looked really good on TV when the Titans scored and everyone waved them around.

Jeff and Ashley stopped at the concession area to get some beers and headed to their seats. When they sat down, Jeff handed Ashley her drink.

"There you go," he said.

"Thanks," she said. "My dad always says there's nothing better than beer and hockey." Jeff chuckled at her comment.

"Yeah my dad always said stuff like that, too." The players finished their warm-up skate and the announcer built up the crowd before the game started. The red towels waved all across the stands. The puck dropped and they cheered the Titans on. The game was filled with excitement with lots of back and forth action and big hits. Every now and then, the beer guy came around and shouted out his offerings. Jeff asked if Ashley wanted any more.

"Ugh, it's so expensive here," she said. Jeff gave her a look filled with anger.

"What? You think I can't afford it?" She looked back at him with wide eyes.

"No, Jeff, that's not—"

"Sorry," Jeff cut in. "Long day. It's my treat."

He waved his hand to dismiss his own comment.

"I'd love one. Thanks," she said. Right after they got their drinks, the Titans got a breakaway on a bad line change and some fancy skating by their hottest defenseman, Robbie Lawson. He deked left, then right, then backhanded the puck over the goalie's glove and in the net. The red light came on and the horn blared out. The arena exploded with cheering. Jeff and Ashley jumped up out of their seats. In the excitement, Jeff spilled some beer on the bald head of the man in front of him. He noticed right away and tapped him on the shoulder.

"Sorry, man," he said through the noise. Jeff offered him his red towel. The man was upset at first but he was nice about it.

"No harm done," he said and turned back around. He used his own towel to dry off and Jeff looked at Ashley. He shrugged his shoulders and smiled. She put her hand over her mouth to stop the laughter.

The period ended and they both went outside to have a cigarette. On the way back, they stopped at the concession again for more beer and got to their seats just in time for the second period to start.

The game picked up right where it left off and there was a lot of rough stuff after the whistles. The Titans had a speedy little guy named Ellison. He was behind the goal line and went from side to side to try and shake his defender. He made his move but the Bulls player stuck his leg and tripped him up. The crowd roared with disapproval as the visiting team made their way up the ice with no penalty called on the play.

"What the fuck, referee?" Jeff yelled out. Ashley tugged on Jeff's shirt to get him to sit back down. The bald man turned to look at Jeff but he paid him no mind. The Bulls ended up scoring on the play and arena was filled with a chorus of boos. When the crowd settled, Jeff stood up to further his complaint.

"That's bullshit, ref!" he said. The bald man stood up and turned to face Jeff.

"Hey watch your language, boy-o," he said. "My kids are here."

"Boy-o?" Jeff said. "Who you calling boy-o, old man?"

"Jeff, come on. Let's just watch the game," Ashley said as she motioned for him to sit back down.

"Look. Just cool down, alright?" the man said.

"Cool down. That's a good idea," Jeff said. He poured his beer on the bald man's head and threw his cup on the ground.

"Jeff, stop it!" Ashley said. The man stood there, frozen, with a stunned look on his face. Just then, two large men in yellow shirts with security printed on the front and back had come down to their section of seats.

"Sir," the bigger of the two said, "we're going to have to ask you to come with us." Jeff looked at Ashley and gave her a smug smile.

"Unbelievable," he said as he threw his hands in the air. Jeff looked at the beer soaked man in front of him one last time and tossed his red towel in his face before he turned and left.

"C'mon, Ash," he said and shuffled toward the end of the aisle. She followed and whispered an apology to the bald man as she gave him her towel on the way by. When security led them out, the small section of the crowd who had witnessed the incident gave a little applause and returned their attention to the game.

Jeff walked side by side with the bigger guard and the smaller, but still very large one, walked behind him. Ashley walked with small, quick steps to try and keep up with them. They were taken to a small security office where the yellow shirted men took Jeff's picture then escorted him out of the building. On the street, Jeff finally spoke up.

"Well, want to go see my friend play a show at the pub?" he said as he pointed in the direction of The Golden Fleece. Ashley looked at her watch.

"Thanks, Jeff but I think I'm gonna head home," she said. He looked at her like she was crazy to refuse.

"Your loss," he said and turned to go. He smoked a cigarette as he walked to the bar. When he arrived, Colin was almost ready to go on stage.

"Oi, Jeff," he said. "Game over already?"

"Nah, some old asshole tried to start a fight with me and I got kicked out. Can you believe that?"

"Shitty," Colin said. He looked around the bar. "Where's your lady friend?"

"She went home," Jeff said. "That chick is whack. I think she just went with me for the free ticket, ya know?"

"Ah, who needs her then? Have a drink, mate." Colin pointed to the bar. Jeff didn't need any convincing. He had a few drinks while Colin played his songs. About an hour later, Brody came in and joined Jeff at the bar.

"Sup, cockface?" he said and sat down.

"Brody..." Jeff said and raised his glass to greet him. "Shots?" Jeff said. Brody slapped his hands on the bar and made a loud whooping noise.

"Let's get fuckin' messy!" he said. "Oh Jeff, did you see that Titans game?" Jeff laughed through his nose.

"No, Brody," he said. "Not all of it."

After that, Jeff's memory blurred and the next thing he remembered was waking up at home. He opened his burning eyes to the harsh morning light. He rose from bed and tried to fill in the blanks. The first thing he thought about was Ashley. He couldn't believe that she blew him off like that. *What a bitch,* he thought. He knew it would be weird at work but they didn't cross paths too much so he wasn't worried about it much. He couldn't shake the heavy feeling in his head. He went to the kitchen and poured himself a glass of coke. He looked at it like something was missing. He opened the freezer and grabbed his bottle of vodka. His father's voice rang through his head. *Best cure for a hangover, boy-o.*

Jeff kept to his usual routine for the rest of the week. He did his best to avoid Ashley at work and he figured she did the same. The manager had scheduled a staff meeting for Friday night and everyone was required to go. The boss, Terry, told everyone to meet at the bar & grill across the street and that dinner was on him. Jeff stopped at the liquor store on his way there and bought a big bottle of vodka. He got to the meeting early and bought a double vodka and coke at the bar. He joined everyone at the big table when they arrived. He made sure to sit as far away from Ashley as he could. Terry told them about some changes in the menu and special promotions that were on their way. Jeff didn't pay much attention, though. He excused himself and went to the bathroom. On his way back, he bought another drink from the bar.

The business talk ended and everyone chatted while they ate. Jeff nibbled at his food and excused himself again to hit the bar. By the time they wrapped things up, Jeff was all smiles.

"OK, guys," Terry said. "Thanks for coming. Have a great shift." Jeff had a smoke on his way back across the street and got changed before they opened the doors. It was a slow night and every now and then Jeff slipped into the break room and took a swig from his bottle that he stashed away in his bag. He bumped against Terry on his way back and fell over.

"Jesus, Jeff. Are you alright?" Terry said as he helped him up.

"Yeah I'm good, boss." Terry sniffed the air as he straightened his blazer.

"You sure?"

"Yep. Feeling good."

"Good. Can you do me a favour? We need some more steaks out of the cooler."

"I'm on it," Jeff said. He got the tray from the cooler and carried it back to the kitchen. He whistled a tune while he walked. Jeff stumbled and dropped the tray of steaks. The tray clanged on the floor and the steaks slid along the tile. Terry was still in the hallway.

"Oh for God's sake, Jeff," he said.

"Oh man. It was an accident, boss."

"Damn it, Jeff. I tried to look the other way

but you know we have a zero tolerance policy here."

"What?"

"You're drunk. I can smell it on you."

"Terry—"

"Save it," Terry said. "You're fired. Grab your stuff and get out of here."

"Fine." Jeff changed his clothes and grabbed his bag from the break room. Terry walked him out the back door. Jeff walked home fast. He was angry with himself but at least he didn't have to tiptoe around Ashley anymore.

Jeff found a job at a new restaurant about a week later. He didn't tell them that he had been fired, just that he wanted something new. He figured they were desperate for experienced cooks and used it to his advantage. He knew he lucked out when they didn't ask for any references.

CHAPTER SIX
To Thine Own Self Be True

Today

Jeff put the Titans jersey back in the closet. He was about to turn away and close the door but something caught his eye on the top shelf. A tiny metallic glimmer from a small shoebox. It had a little bronze decoration with a rectangular space in the middle to label it. The label was handwritten and it was just one word. Leetch. He reached up and took it down. It was a bit too dark in his mom's room so he brought it to the kitchen near the big window. He poured another drink while he was at it and opened the box.

It was full of little things. Mementoes, he supposed. There were some small Polaroids and letters from family. The heavier things were underneath. Jeff saw his mom's wedding bands and some newspaper clippings. He was going to read them but then he saw some big coins. They were all different colours. He took them out, one by one. On the front of each coin was a number inside a triangle. One of the sides of the triangle were the words unity, service and recovery. There was an inscription around the edge, too. To thine own self be true. There were seven coins, all different colours and different numbers. Jeff held up the blue one. They weren't coins at all. His mom must have gone to Alcoholics Anonymous at some point and these were her sobriety chips. As far as he could tell, she made it six months. He wondered how long ago it was, though, because her freezer was full of booze. He turned the chip over. It had some small writing on the back.

God grant me the serenity to accept the things I cannot change, courage to change things I can and wisdom to know the difference. Jeff remembered where he had heard the before.

9 years ago

Jeff was twenty-five years old and finally bought his first car. He was at The Golden Fleece telling Colin and Brody all about it.

"Sounds sweet, Jeffy," Brody said. "You know what this means, right?" Brody looked around the pub like he was about to whisper a secret.

Instead, he yelled out as loud as he could. "Road trip!" They all laughed. Jeff thought it was a good idea. Brody said they could go to his dad's cabin.

"Best bit of all, last call is whenever we bloody like," Colin said.

"Fuckin' right, man," Brody said. "Jeff, I'll load my pickup with beers. Your ride hauls the luggage and supplies."

"Let's do it," Jeff said. They decided the coming weekend was the perfect time. They were all off work and had no plans. Colin was in charge of the music and Jeff would handle the food. They drank the rest of the night away and talked about how great it was going to be.

The next couple of days went by and the weekend had arrived. Jeff loaded up his car with the groceries. It was mostly burgers and sausages for the grill. Brody had given them the directions and he would meet them there. Jeff closed the trunk and went to pick up Colin. When Jeff arrived, Colin was waiting on his front porch with his bags and a big leather album of CDs.

"Some tunes for the road?" Colin said and patted the booklet.

"For sure," Jeff said. Colin put in a Pink Floyd disc and turned up the volume. They were almost at the end of the album when they reached the cabin. Jeff spotted Brody's truck parked in front. The cabin was in a secluded area. Trees lined the driveway and blocked out the sun. The cabin was surrounded by woods except for a small clearing behind it that led to a sandy little beach. It was isolated, too. They were about a twenty minute drive from the nearest town. Brody popped his head out from the screen door and yelled out to them.

"You two lovebirds have a nice drive?" he said. He pursed his lips and made kissing sound.

"Yeah, yeah," Jeff said. "Come help with all this shit." When they unloaded the car Brody took them to his pickup truck. He stopped before they got there and smiled at Colin and Jeff.

"You ready for this?" Brody said. He took them around to the back of the blue truck and showed them their fuel for the weekend. Jeff stood in awe of what was before him. The entire truck was filled with beer and liquor. Everyone's favourites were there.

"Damn, Brody," Jeff said. "Are you sure you got enough?" They all laughed and unloaded the truck together. When they got it all in, Brody grabbed each of them a beer and pointed his bottle at Colin as he swallowed a mouthful.

"Tunes, man," he said. "We need some tunes."

"Right," Colin said and grabbed his booklet.

"No artsy-fartsy stuff," Brody said. He looked

at Jeff. "I ain't drunk enough for the shit. Not yet." Jeff smiled and they clinked their bottles together. Colin put on some Zeppelin and cranked it up. They had a few beers on the back deck in the afternoon sun. They talked about their plans for the weekend. Colin told them about the brilliance of Jimmy Page. Brody boasted about his various sexual escapades in graphic detail. They all had a good laugh and told stories. After a few hours, Brody fired up the grill and cooked some up sausages. They planned to have a big bonfire in the open area near the lake. After dinner they gathered some wood and kindling and built a great mountain of branches and logs. Brody brought out some lawn chairs that had cup holders built in to the arm rests. Jeff and Colin carried out a big cooler full of ice and beer bottles. There were cans of coke to mix with the vodka and whiskey that Jeff carried in his free hand. When they put everything down Brody was standing with his hands on his hips, admiring the towering pile of wood before him. He turned around when he heard Jeff and Colin put down the cooler.

"They'll be able to see this son of a bitch from space," he said. He clapped his hands and ran back to the cabin. He came back out carrying an extension cord and the boom box in one arm and Colin's music collection in the other.

"Ah, brilliant," Colin said and took the book

from him. "What shall it be, lads?"

"Drinking music," Jeff said. Colin thumbed through his collection and held his choice up in the air.

"Journey. Classic," he said. They drank and sang along to the music. Colin played air guitar. The sun had almost gone down and they were having a great time. The cooler looked a bit empty so Jeff went back to the cabin to grab some more drinks. He carried what he could in his arms and when he got back to the bonfire he heard unfamiliar voices. Brody and Colin were talking with some people. Brody noticed Jeff had returned and made the introductions.

"Hey this is Jeff," he said. "Jeff, this is Dan, Matt, and Vicky." He pointed at them as he said their names.

"Nice to meet you," Jeff said as he put the drinks in the cooler. He noticed a boat tied up at the edge of the water.

"This lot has a cabin on the other side of the lake," Colin said. "They saw the fire and—"

"No shit they saw it," Brody interrupted. The newcomers laughed at Brody. Matt, the tall one, spoke up.

"Thought the house was on fire," he said and chuckled. "So we grabbed the boat and rowed on over to check on it."

"Figured they might as well join the party now that they're here, hey Jeff?" Brody said.

"The more the merrier," Jeff said as he moved his hand toward the cooler to offer them a drink. The truth was, Jeff never believed that old saying. He preferred familiar faces or isolation if anything, but these people didn't seem too bad. They talked about the usual things. What they did for a living, plans for the weekend and the like. Matt and Vicky were brother and sister. Dan was Matt's friend from college. Vicky was going off to Australia for school in the fall. Some sort of interior design thing. Her parents had been cramming in as many family events that they could think of before she went away. The sun had set and the only light came from the enormous fire they were gathered around. Colin was startled by every little noise in the surrounding woods.

"Bloody hell, man. I'll be eaten alive," he said.

"Calm down, princess," Brody said. "It's just critters."

"Critters? Bit vague, innit?" Colin said and turned to Vicky. "We don't even have skunks in England, you know."

"Oh stop it," she said.

"No, it's true," he said and peered out to the darkness with a theatrical, worried look on his face. "I'm not cut out for the wild kingdom." Everyone laughed at the joke and Vicky slapped him on the back.

"I'll protect you, tough guy," she said and

they laughed again. They drank for a few hours and the newcomers thanked the guys for the drinks. They got in their boat and rowed back across the lake. After they left, Colin grabbed a new album and put it on. It was a mix he had made of what Brody would call artsy-fartsy stuff. They smoked and drank while the fire died down. The album ended, the fire was reduced to embers, and they decided to call it a night. They kicked sand on the remains of the once raging inferno and gathered their things. Inside, Jeff opened a bag of chips and ate a handful before he offered some to the others. He poured a vodka and coke into a party cup.

"Anybody else want one?" he said. They both declined and Colin stumbled toward his room.

"I'm spent," he said. "Night all." Brody grunted something at him and dragged his feet all the way to his room. Jeff shrugged his shoulders and sat down with his drink on an old chair in the main room. He must have been tired because he woke up the next morning in the same spot. The smell of bacon being cooked filled his nose. Brody was in the kitchen and saw Jeff stretch himself awake.

"Wakey wakey, eggs and bakey," he said. Colin shuffled out of the bathroom like a zombie.

"Oh. My. God." he said.

"Morning, sunshine," Brody said as he

opened two bottles of beer and put them on the counter for his friends. "Hair of the dog, fuckers," he said. They sat on the bar stools lined up at the counter and clinked their bottles together. Brody gave them each a plate of eggs, bacon, and breakfast sausages. They all ate and drank their beer. The planned to go swimming that day. Their new friends from the night before told them that they would be setting off fireworks from the other side of the lake that night and they were welcome to join. After breakfast, they had a beer on the patio and got their things together for a swim. They walked down to the edge of the water. Their monstrous bonfire from the night before was nothing but a pile of ashes and blackened pieces of wood.

"We'll clean that shit up later," Brody said. He pointed to a raft anchored in the middle of the lake. Jeff wondered who the hell had put it there and why they did it. Maybe for fishing or just relaxing like they had planned to do.

They loaded Brody's tiny little wood boat with their booze and towels. Colin sat in the middle of the boat with his collapsible chair on his lap so Jeff and Brody had to do the rowing. They paddled out to the raft and tied the boat to it. Colin climbed out with extreme caution and the others followed. The square raft was like a big back porch with a ladder attached to it instead of a house. They set up shop and had a beer before Jeff and Brody decided to have a swim. Colin sat in his chair and enjoyed his drink. The small waves created by their swimming caused the raft to rock a bit. Once they had their fill, they returned to the raft and Brody hoisted himself up. It caused the raft to lift up the side that Colin was on. When it lowered back down, he tumbled backward in his chair and his limbs flailed about. He fell in the water with a huge splash. His head popped back up and he grasped the edge of the raft.

"I've lost my beer," Colin said as he wiped the water from his face. Brody was on his hands and knees, doubled over with laughter.

"That was the funniest fucking thing I've ever seen!" he said. Jeff got on the raft and helped Colin up. He was laughing too hard to be of much help and Colin joined in. After they were all safely aboard again, they had some more drinks and soaked in the sun before they headed back to dry land.

In the house, Jeff went to his room and changed his clothes. He took a few swigs from his bottle of vodka that he had stashed in the dresser drawer and went to the kitchen. Brody was getting ready to grill something for lunch. Jeff made them all a strong vodka and coke and they sat out on the porch while their burgers cooked. Brody finished grilling and they ate their lunch outside.

"There's a store in town that sells fireworks," Brody said. "We should get some for tonight. Add to the show, you know?"

"Sounds awesome," Jeff said. "I'll go grab a bunch."

"You alright to drive, mate?" Colin said.

"Oh yeah," Jeff said as he rubbed his stomach. "Those burgers did the trick." He went back inside and grabbed his keys from the dresser in his room. He took a big drink from his secret bottle while he was at it. The others had come back in and, as Jeff was on his way out, Brody had a last minute request.

"Jeff, grab some more ice for the cooler," he said. Without turning around, Jeff pointed a finger in the air to confirm. He got in his car and turned it around to head out. He drove down the winding country road and felt very content. It was already a great weekend and that night was shaping up to be even better. He passed a few dirt path driveways that led to other cabins in the area. He must have been looking too long because he didn't see the sharp bend in the road until it was too late. He jerked the wheel but his tire was in the dirt of the shoulder and the back end of the car slid the wrong way. He tried to correct himself but he yanked the wheel too far the other way. He slammed both feet on the brake pedal but his tires slid in the dirt. He saw the tree trunk he was headed for and the last thing he remembered was coming to a loud, hard stop before his head whipped toward the window.

CHAPTER SEVEN
28 Days

Jeff woke up in terrible pain. Blinding light poured into the room. His head was throbbing. His eyes took a moment to clear and he looked around the room. He was in a bed but it wasn't his. His forehead stung and he lifted his right hand to touch it but it was stopped with a clang of metal on metal. He looked down at his wrist. It was handcuffed to the metal railing on the side of the... hospital bed. It all came rushing back to him. He was in a car accident and he was drunk. Now he was handcuffed to a bed in a hospital. An IV was stuck in the top of his hand. He looked around the room and tried to ignore the pain in his head. He squinted from the harsh sun and his forehead only hurt more. He lifted his left hand but it felt heavy. He looked and saw that his forearm was covered in a big white cast.

"Christ," he said. He touched his forehead and felt what he assumed were stitches. It stung when he touched them and he winced in pain. He let out a sigh. *How did I let this happen?* Jeff thought. *Idiot.* It was his first offence but it was a big one. He wondered what kind of shape his car was in. It couldn't be great considering the damage his body took. He sat there thinking. He let the memories fill in the blanks of the day before. Was it the day before? How long had he been there? His head pounded. Just then, the nurse walked in.

"Rise and shine, Mr. Leetch," she said as she looked at her clipboard. "My name is Patty. Let me tell you what happened." Jeff cleared his throat and croaked out a question.

"What day is it?" he said.

"You had an accident yesterday, Mr. Leetch," she said.

"Jeff."

"I'm sorry?"

"You can... you can call me Jeff," he said.

"OK. You had an accident yesterday. Police brought you in. You were in rough shape. Let's see here." She looked at her clipboard again. "Broken ulna, laceration on forehead. You got 12 stitches for that one. A concussion and bumps and bruises all over. You might not feel it now but your leg is going to be very sore for the next little while." Jeff moved the blanket to show his left thigh. It was bright red and covered in small cuts.

"Yep," Patty said, "lucky it didn't break, too." She checked the IV bags that led to the needle in his hand and made some notes on her chart.

"When do I get out of here?" Jeff said. Patty stopped her work, let out a small breath and grabbed Jeff's right hand. The handcuff clanged against the bed rail.

"Whenever they think you're well enough," she said and put his hand back down. She showed him the call button and told him that food would be coming soon. On her way out, she turned back to face him.

"Oh, I almost forgot," she said. "It's Sunday." She went out to the nurses station and Jeff laid his head back down on the bed. He wondered what Brody and Colin had thought. He was just popping over to grab some fireworks but never came back. He looked around the room again. He saw a white plastic bag with a drawstring on a chair in the corner. The words Personal Belongings were printed on it in big blue letters. He wondered if his cigarettes were in there. He knew he wouldn't be able to have one, though. Not while he was chained up to the bed.

He shut his eyes to try and ease the pain in his head. He tried to shut out the thoughts in his mind. He wondered how long he would be there and how badly he would be punished. He wondered how he was supposed to— He snapped out of it and hit the call nurse button.

"Yes, Mr. Leetch?" the voice said.

"How am I supposed to... use the bathroom?" His voice lowered at the end.

"Silver pan, bedside table. Someone will collect it soon." Jeff looked at the bedpan and sighed.

"Thanks," he said.

His lunch came a short while later but he wasn't hungry. He drank the juice and water and an orderly collected his tray. He closed his eyes and drifted off to sleep.

He woke up covered in cold sweat. He wasn't out long, according to the clock on the wall. He could see a police officer stationed outside his door. He scribbled answers on a newspaper crossword. Jeff groaned and stretched but his hand was still cuffed to the bed. The policeman looked over his shoulder at Jeff when he heard the cuffs ring against the rail. He stood up and put his paper on the chair.

"Mr. Leetch, my name is Sargeant Mills. Here's what happened. Your vehicle left the road and hit a tree. Lucky for you, your friends got worried and went looking for you. They called 911 when they found you unconscious. Ambulance brought you here and we ordered a toxicology screen. Your blood alcohol content was over the legal limit. At the crash site, a silver flask was found inside the vehicle. You are being charged with driving under the influence of alcohol, driving with an open alcohol container and reckless driving. You will see a judge in the morning by video conference. Until then, I'll be right out there." Mills finished and unlocked the handcuffs. "All of this will be provided in writing soon. Do you understand?" Jeff nodded. "Don't make things worse for yourself," Mills said. "Just stay in here." He went out and sat in his chair to finish his puzzle.

Jeff rested his head and sat in silence for the rest of the day. He drifted in and out of sleep. His nurse had said that the drugs would make him tired. Each time he woke it took him a moment to remember where he was. In the morning he was given breakfast and he ate a little. Jeff heard the radio on Mills' shoulder squawk something out and he wheeled in a stand with a small TV and camera on it. He plugged it in and waited next to it. A skinny man came in and plugged in some wires to a gadget and the screen lit up. On the screen, Jeff saw a small courtroom and some people waiting and getting ready for the day. Some nervous teenagers tried to look respectable in their shirts and ties. Jeff wondered how he would look. Broken, battered, and bruised in his hospital bed. The bailiff announced the arrival of Judge

Riker who called the court to order. Jeff had to wait while the nervous teenagers had their punishment delivered. Community service for shoplifting. They left the room and the judge called the next case.

"Jeff Leetch," he said. Jeff perked up on his bed.

"Yes, sir." His heart pounded and his stomach churned.

"Have you been read your charges?" Riker said.

"I have, sir."

"Driving under the influence of alcohol, driving with an open alcohol container and reckless driving," the judge read from his file. "How do you plead?" Jeff responded without hesitating.

"Guilty, sir." Riker looked up from his file and fixed his gaze on the camera.

"I've reviewed your case. You will complete a twenty-eight day rehabilitation program effective immediately upon your release from the hospital. If you fail to complete the program, I will not hesitate to give you jail time. Do you understand, Mr. Leetch?"

"Yes, sir."

"Sargeant Mills will provide you with documentation. Dismissed," Riker said.

"Thank you, sir," Jeff said. The skinny technician unplugged the equipment and left.

Mills wrote something on his notepad and told Jeff that he would be back with the paperwork. Jeff breathed a sigh of exhaustion and relief. He knew he had gotten off easy but his mind reeled from what had just happened. *Twenty-eight days,* he thought. He wondered what would happen to his job and his apartment. He wondered if Colin and Brody would help take care of things for him. He wondered where the hell they were. They found him in a car wreck and hadn't even come to visit. Maybe he wasn't allowed visitors. Maybe they did come but got stopped by his guard dog, Mills.

Jeff spent the next few days staring out the window and had some minor treatment from the nurses. Colin and Brody stopped by, too. Jeff was right. They told him he wasn't allowed to have visitors until after his court appearance unless it was his lawyer. They talked about the car crash and how court went. Sargeant Mills dropped off the paperwork and had Jeff sign a few things. Brody offered to drive Jeff to rehab. Jeff gave Colin the keys to his apartment so he could collect his mail. The nurse told him that he would be released later that day. He had to go directly to the rehab facility that was just outside the city. Brody came back with a backpack full of Jeff's clothes in his hand.

"Ready to roll, Jeffy?" he said.

"Yeah, lemme change first," Jeff said. He got

dressed in the bathroom.

"D'you get all your shit?" Brody said.

"Yep. Let's bust out of here."

They drove out to the rehab centre without saying much to each other. Jeff confirmed the time and date that Brody had to pick him up. They pulled up to a dark, wood building that looked like a log cabin from the front. It was dimly lit by a little yellow bulb above the front steps.

"You good?" Brody said.

"Yep. Thanks, man," Jeff said.

"Anytime."

"See ya." Jeff closed the door and headed up the steps to the building. He was greeted by a skinny, bug-eyed man with grey hair that crept up the sides of his head.

"Jeff, welcome to The Greenstone Centre," he said.

"Hey. Jeff Leetch."

"Come on in and we'll get you settled, Jeff."

"Sure. Nice to meet you, Mr.—"

"Frank," he said. "Only first names here." Frank took him to a small office. He sat in front of a big bookshelf full of self help manuals and inspirational books. Frank went over the rules and Jeff felt like this guy would never stop. They talked for what felt like forever. Rules, group therapy, activities, and more rules. Jeff had to turn in his keys and his flask. He just left everything in his personal effects bag from the hospital. Frank gave Jeff a tour of the facility. There was a bank machine and a variety store on the grounds. The first floor was mostly therapy rooms and recreation areas. The bedrooms were on the second floor. Behind the house there was a huge field. There were benches, picnic tables and little gardens here and there. A small lake glistened in the setting sun and Jeff spotted a little wood boat by the tiny dock.

"Yep," Frank said, "it's real peaceful here." Frank showed him upstairs to his room and introduced him to his roommate. "This is Ricky. Ricky, this is Jeff."

"Hey, man," Ricky said. He laid on his bed, reading a book. He was the skinniest guy that Jeff had ever seen. His bones poked out from his skin and his arms were covered in little puncture wounds.

"Hey," Jeff said. Frank pointed to Jeff's nightstand.

"There's a schedule in the top drawer for you. Come on down anytime if you have any questions." Frank left and Jeff sat on the edge of his bed. He took out the booklet and flipped through it mindlessly. He saw Ricky put his book down.

"Psst, hey," Ricky said. "What ya in for?" Jeff looked up.

"DUI," he said. Ricky nodded his head. Jeff

could tell that Ricky wanted to talk. "How about you?"

"Man," Ricky said and exhaled. "Intervention." He held his arms out toward Jeff. "Smack." Jeff nodded. "Yep, uncle said he'd call the cops on me if I didn't go along."

"Damn."

"Yep. Not so bad here, though," Ricky said. He waved his book at Jeff. "Gotta keep yourself busy, though, or you'll go bonkers."

"Maybe I'll take a little walk around," Jeff said.

"I'll be here. Seeya, man."

"Later."

Jeff walked around the facility and checked out the different rooms. The shop was closed but it looked like they had cigarettes behind the counter. When he got back to his room, Ricky was passed out with his book on his chest. Jeff turned off the nightstand lamp and wound the old fashioned alarm clock so he would have plenty of time to get himself ready in the morning. He was exhausted. It was mental fatigue more than physical and when he laid his head on the pillow, he nodded off.

The alarm rang out its awful sound and Jeff shot awake. He was covered in cold sweat but it wasn't like usual. His hands shook and his head pounded. He had forgotten about his head injury until he pressed his hand against his forehead and felt the stitches. He smacked the alarm clock until it stopped clanging and sat on the edge of his bed. He looked over his schedule for the day and got himself ready. Thankfully, his first stop every morning was medication. He folded up his schedule and put it in his back pocket. As he went down the stairs he saw his bug-eyed tour guide waiting for him.

"Good morning, Jeff," he said.

"Oh hi, Mr.—" Jeff had forgotten his name.

"Frank."

"Right. Sorry, Mr. Frank," Jeff said. Frank chuckled and Jeff apologized when he realized his error. Frank waved his hand in forgiveness.

"Heck, I've been called worse. How'd you sleep?" he said.

"Not bad, all things considered," Jeff said as he pulled his schedule out of his back pocket. "Can you point me in the right direction?" Frank looked at the paper.

"Let me show you," he said and they walked together. Frank showed him where he could find the places he needed to be that day and they ended up at the dispensary. An old nurse stood behind the sliding glass of the high counter. Frank introduced them.

"New recruit, huh?"

"Yep," Jeff said. "Can I get something for my arm?" he said and showed her his cast. She rolled her eyes at Frank and breathed in through her nose before she answered.

"This ain't pick your poison, sweetie," she said. "Hospital gave you what you needed while you were there. Medical report didn't prescribe anything for you. So you'll get only what you need while you're here." She shook a bottle of aspirin at him and smiled as she handed him the little plastic cup with two pills in it. "I'll bet you've got some aches and pains, though. Here you go," she said and gave him a paper cup filled with water. Jeff accepted her terms and took his pills.

"Come on, Jeff," said Frank as he led them away. "Just grab some aspirin at the store later." They parted ways at the cafeteria and Jeff got a bagel and some juice. He turned around and looked for an empty table when he spotted Ricky. He was waving his hands like one of those guys at the airport who guided the planes in. The table was almost full and Jeff didn't feel much like socializing but he joined them anyway. He didn't want to be rude so he sat down and smiled. Ricky introduced everyone at the table and what problem they were in for. They were a mix of poppers, shooters, boozers, and snorters. Some of them had more than one vice. They were all in the same group therapy sessions and sort of stuck together in their free time.

"Peeked at your schedule, dude. You're gonna be with us in group," Ricky said.

"Cool," Jeff said. He wasn't used to chatting with strangers without a drink in his hand at a bar. He remembered the TV in the lounge from his tour the night before and stuck to a safe topic.

"Anybody catch the score of the Titans game last night?" he said. They all shook their heads to say no. The older woman, whose name escaped him already, told Jeff they had watched a movie the night before.

"Gone With The Wind," she said. "Such a good one, don't you think?"

"Never seen it," Jeff said.

"Oh, you should watch it."

"Will do," Jeff said. They finished their breakfast and Ricky showed Jeff the chore board. Everyone had a different task and it changed every couple of days. Jeff had to stock the refrigerators for the rest of the week. He had to lug everything up from the big walk-in cooler in the basement.

Every trip up and down the stairs left him breathless. He finished his work and had a cigarette in the smoking area. There were people scattered around the grounds outside. Some did yoga. Some read by themselves. Others just walked and talked. Jeff had some time before his group session so he browsed the library for anything interesting he could read in his free time at night. They mostly had self-help books.

There were a few classics. Jeff grabbed a few and dropped them off in his room.

He made his way to the group therapy room and found Ricky already waiting. The therapist came in with the rest of the group. They did introductions for Jeff's benefit. After everyone had repeated what he already heard at breakfast, it was his turn. He cleared his throat and began.

"My name is Jeff," he said, "and I'm here on court order for drunk driving." He made it a point not to say that he was an alcoholic. He was in control of his drinking. He only had a car accident. The fact that he forgot about his flask and the winding roads were what landed him at Greenstone. The others nodded and officially welcomed him. The therapist, Gloria, started the session with some recaps and got updates from the rest of the group on their progress. Jeff listened to their tales carefully and paid special attention to the type of things that seemed to please Gloria. She turned to Jeff and asked him to share his story. He described the crash as he remembered it and glazed over the legal part of the story. Gloria thanked him with a bow of her head.

"How often do you drink, Jeff?" she said. Jeff looked to the ceiling and thought for a moment.

"Not much, really," he said.

"How much is not much?"

"I don't know." He shrugged his shoulders.

"Tell us about your typical week."

"Well, let's see. I work in a kitchen during the week," Jeff said.

"What do you like to do after work?"

"I don't know. Watch TV or hang out with friends."

"Where?" Gloria said.

"Uhh," Jeff stalled He realized the only answer was The Golden Fleece or some other bar. He tried to think of something else but nothing came. "I guess, now that I think of it..." he stopped and looked at Ricky. He gave Jeff an assuring nod to continue. "The bar."

"And what about the weekends?" Gloria didn't let up.

"Yeah, the same," Jeff said. He wasn't ashamed but felt some sense of pity from the others in the group.

"Do you ever drink alone?"

"Yeah, I guess. Sometimes," he lied. He waited for Gloria continue her interrogation but she just looked at him. He shifted in his chair, uncomfortable in silence.

"You know, at the end of a long day, watching a movie. That kind of thing. Not often, though," Jeff said and looked at the others. They all just nodded and listened. He felt like they could see right through him but wouldn't call him out for not telling the truth. Thankfully, Gloria spoke.

"Thanks, Jeff," she said. "It's helpful to

examine your life this way so you can see it the way others might." He slumped back in his chair. He hadn't realized how tense he had become during the exchange. "Thanks for sharing," Gloria said. The group echoed her appreciation. They ended the session and headed out for lunch. After he ate, Jeff went to the store and bought some cigarettes and aspirin. Ricky was already there, stocking up on junk food. After that, it was time for individual therapy. It was a continuation of how group was. Jeff was just as defensive and dishonest as earlier.

He maintained his stance throughout his stay at Greenstone. He wasn't a drunk. He made a mistake and left his flask in the car. Jeff learned to mirror the things that the others would say so he could appease his therapists. He suspected they knew that he was just going through the motions but they never called him out. He figured they didn't want to waste their energy on a court ordered case over someone who really, truly wanted to kick the habit. Ricky, for example, really did want to stop using. They would talk at night instead of reading those self-help books filled with inspirational quotes. It was Ricky's second time in rehab. He was clean for three months the first time around.

"What happened?" Jeff said. Ricky took a deep breath and cocked his head before he answered.

"Shit," he said and looked back at Jeff. "I guess it was a bunch of stuff all at once. I mean, I tried to stay friends with guys who were still using and just not be around at party time, ya know?"

"But..." Jeff said.

"But I got laid off, my girl skipped out on me and my dad died all in the same week."

"Damn."

"Yeah. I just couldn't deal with it all so I hit up my boys and instead of leaving when they brought out the junk, I stayed. The rest is history, ya know?" Ricky said and looked down at his toes.

"Yeah," Jeff said and nodded.

"You know what's fucked up, though?" Ricky looked at him again.

"What's that?"

"My friends," he said. "It's like they were happy for me. 'Welcome back, Ricky.' Like I was just pretending to be a normal person and the real me was coming back out to play."

"Hmm," Jeff said.

"Anyway, I was right back at it. Couple months later, my uncle had enough and pulled one of those intervention deals. Just like on TV." Ricky laughed.

"Sounds intense," Jeff said even though he didn't understand the reference.

"Yeah. It was the push I needed, though," he said. "I wanted to stop but never had a good reason. I sure as hell don't wanna go to the bighouse." Ricky paused to flip through a book on his bed. "And, there's no such thing as an old junkie." He showed the page to Jeff and smiled, showing as many teeth as possible. They both laughed. Jeff admired Ricky for wanting to quit the habit. He couldn't imagine a needle in his arm and Ricky's stories made him glad he never got into drugs.

The days turned to weeks. Some new people came to stay at Greenstone. Ricky and a few others from the group eventually graduated and were sent back to the real world. Ricky was set to stay at a sober house for a while and gave Jeff the address so he could come by and visit when he got out. Jeff never did get another roommate before his graduation. Those last few nights were pretty boring without the sound of candy wrappers crinkling or the sound of Ricky tossing and turning all night long. Blanket on, blanket off. Roll to the left, roll to the right. Flip the pillow, hit the bathroom and start all over again. On Jeff's last night at Greenstone he had trouble falling asleep. He thought of restless Ricky and smiled. He decided he would have to stop in and see how Ricky was doing sometime.

Jeff woke up before his alarm and started to pack his things. Brody was due to pick him up after breakfast. He ate with what was left his group.

They didn't talk much. They always seemed a little sad when someone left but they put on a happy face and said their goodbyes. It was finally Jeff's turn and he couldn't wait to get back home. He finished his breakfast and headed back up to his room to gather the rest of his things. As he closed the door, he stopped to look at the empty room. There was nothing special about the single beds or the plain night tables. The unremarkable window was covered in unremarkable drawstring blinds. The bathroom was clinical; all function and no form. There was nothing special about the room at all but, in that moment, it felt special to Jeff. He thought about Ricky and checked his bag to make sure he had the address of the sober living house before he shut the door.

Jeff signed out at the front desk and endured the goodbye ritual from his group. Frank walked him out and gave him his business card.

"Just in case," he said. "Good luck, Jeff." Frank held out his hand. Jeff shook it and thanked him before he headed to the truck. Brody smoked in the driver's seat. Jeff tossed his bag in the flatbed and got in.

"Ready?" Brody said.

"Yep."

"Straight home?"

"Nah, let's celebrate," Jeff said as he buckled his belt. "Golden Fleece?"

"Good to have you back, fucker." Brody put the truck in gear and pulled away.

CHAPTER EIGHT
Ricky

Four or five weeks had gone by before Jeff thought about Ricky again. He had gotten back to his regular routines. To his surprise, he still had his job. His boss was pretty understanding and needed all hands on deck anyway. It was probably easier to look the other way than to train someone brand new. Jeff didn't care what the reason was. On his day off he decided to stop in and see his old Greenstone roommate. He stopped at the store and bought a box of bite-sized Halloween chocolate bars. Ricky had told him that those were his favourite.

Jeff had never been down Sheppard Street before. It was close to the college and the houses were set up to be rented by the room during the school year. He arrived at the address that Ricky had given him. The white house had a green awning and fake shutters. The cement steps were falling apart at the sides. There were two men at the top of the flight. They stopped their conversation when they saw Jeff. He checked the address again to make sure he had the right place.

"Uh hi, guys," Jeff said. He looked down at the paper in his hand and back at the brass numbers behind the two men.

"Looking for someone?" one of them said. Jeff put the paper in his pocket.

"Yeah," he said, "I'm here to see Ricky." Jeff realized that he didn't know Ricky's last name. "Is he back from work yet?" The man on the left leaned close to the other one and sent him in the house.

"You should come inside, fella," he said to Jeff. He held the door open and pointed in. He gestured to the couch in the small living room and Jeff took a seat. There were three other guys sat around an old scratched up coffee table. Jeff placed the box of chocolates on the table in front of him. The other man from the porch came in followed by an older man with grey hair that crept up the sides of his head. He looked at the chocolate bars and smiled. He sat down with a grunt in a recliner across from Jeff.

"Gary Trott," He held out his hand to Jeff.

"Jeff Leetch." He had to lean forward to meet

Gary's grip.

"Glad to meet you, Jeff."

"Likewise," Jeff said. He looked around the room and the others all looked away from him.

"You a friend of Ricky's?" Gary said.

"Sort of." Jeff hesitated to reveal how they met but realized that nobody in that house would judge him. "We met at Greenstone. At... rehab. We were roommates there. I just got out."

"Ahh," Gary said. "Haven't seen him since?"

"Nope. Thought I'd surprise him." Jeff pointed to the candy bars. Gary leaned forward in his chair and put his hands on his knees.

"Listen, Jeff. Ain't no easy way to say this so I'll just say it." He paused to take a long breath in through his nose. "Ricky is dead. He overdosed five days ago. We only just found out ourselves a couple days back." Jeff sank in the couch. His stomach turned at the thought of Ricky laying somewhere with a needle dangling from his vein. He felt the colour drain from his face and he could see the concern in Gary's eyes. He took a deep breath to regain his composure.

"How could he have overdosed?"

"Well," Gary said as he shifted in his chair, "it seems he and his old friends were having a party to celebrate Ricky's birthday. He had a bit too much to drink and must have let his guard down. One thing lead to another and, well, he'd been clean a good while and took too much. His body just couldn't handle it." Jeff could hear that Gary was still talking but the pulse of his heart muddled the words. Gary leaned forward and touched Jeff's leg.

"You alright, fella?" Gary said. "You look a little pale." Jeff gathered himself and stood up.

"Yeah, sorry. I just need some air," he said. Gary followed Jeff out the front door. Jeff lit a cigarette and offered one to Gary. He waved it away.

"Listen, Jeff," he said. "I know this is tough. I've seen it happen too much, myself. I'm sorry you had to find out like this."

"So is there, like, a funeral or something?" Jeff said.

"Not that we know of," Gary said. "We had a little memorial last night. Just told stories, said prayers. Nothing official, though." Jeff finished his cigarette with a quick blast of smoke from his lungs.

"OK. Well thanks, Gary," Jeff said. "I should get back home, though." As Jeff walked to the street, Gary called out to him.

"You left your box inside."

"You guys can have it," Jeff said without looking back. He walked quickly and lit another smoke. He sucked it back fast and lit one more. He walked so fast that he must have looked late for something very important. People on the sidewalk moved out of his way as he passed them. Before Jeff realized where he was headed, he was steps away from The Golden Fleece. He went in and sat at the bar. Colin was already there to set up his sound system.

Jeff woke up in bed the next morning. No matter how hard he tried, he couldn't remember a single thing that happened after he ordered a drink.

CHAPTER NINE
Jessica

Today

Jeff felt a little hungry so he looked through the kitchen cupboards. He ate some cookies as he looked through the other cabinets. There wasn't much there but he did see a coffee mug that he sent his mom one year. It had a Landon College logo on it. That was where Jeff met Jessica.

13 years ago

For the most part, they were inseparable. Jeff liked Jessica because she could keep up with him at a party. They actually met at a party. After they had outlasted everyone there, Jeff walked her home as the sun came up. She gave him a little kiss on the cheek before she went inside and the rest was history. She was also the only girl who didn't run away within five minutes of meeting Brody. She could hang with the boys and wasn't afraid to dish it out either. Jeff knew she was a keeper the first time he brought her to The Golden Fleece.

"So you're the one who's been distracting Jeffy-boy, eh?" Brody said to her. He leaned closer to her like he was about to whisper a secret but still spoke so everyone in the bar could hear. "Aren't you worried you'll catch crabs or something?"

"Why?" Jessica said with a smirk. "You're not coming to bed with us." Colin was in the middle of a sip and spewed his beer back in his glass.

After the school year ended, they got a little apartment together.

Jessica looked for work in her field but, when she couldn't find any full time medical receptionist positions, she settled for a part time rotation at a walk-in clinic three or four days a week. Jeff worked as much as he could at the restaurant so they could afford rent and still have some fun on the weekends. She would make him dinner and they'd go to movies. They had a great time together and never really fought with each other. Most weekends they would go to The Golden Fleece or some clubs to drink and dance. Well, she danced. Jeff would stand next to her and do the best move he knew; sway from side to side.

Jeff wanted to save for a car. If he had a car, he could get a job a better restaurant that wasn't downtown. The more he worked, though, the less Jessica did. She would go out shopping and spend time with her girlfriends. Jeff would sometimes work fifty or sixty hours a week and they still weren't saving anything. He asked her if she could work more hours.

"Economy is bad, sweetie," she said. "Nobody's hiring."

The longer it went on, the more time they spent apart. Jeff usually spent an extra hour after his shift at the bar in the restaurant before he would head home. Their weekend outings had all but stopped. If they did go out together, it was out of pure boredom or social obligation. They had become more like roommates than a young couple in love. After a while, Jessica did start to work more. She would pick up shifts at an after hours clinic and was gone most evenings. Jeff wondered what she was spending her money on as they weren't any better off than before. After a long day in the kitchen, Jeff came home to a note on the fridge.

at work
back by 10
— Jess

Jeff made something to eat and the phone rang. It was Brody.

"Hey, shit licker. What's going on?"

"Absolutely nothing. You?"

"Fuck all, man. You and Jess wanna hit The Fleece?" Brody said. Jeff looked at the note on the fridge as he rinsed his dishes.

"She's working."

"Just the boys, then," Brody said. "I'll pick up prissy pants Hardcastle. Can I park at your building again?"

"Sounds like a plan," Jeff said and hung up. He made himself a stiff drink while he waited for his friends to arrive. He sat on the couch and looked around the empty apartment. It wasn't empty, though. There were the tall black vases filled with fake flowers. Jessica had dragged him to some decor shop to spruce the place up. There were the art prints of rocks and flowers. She got them from a fancy craft store in the north end. There were the knick-knacks in the kitchen and bathroom collected from various places, some artsy items on the side tables. Then there was the bedroom. The enormous closet housed her various outfits. Many of them hadn't ever been worn. The jewellery box on the dresser overflowed with accessories and trinkets. The entire place was hers. Aside from his small sliver of closet space and the top drawer of the dresser, there was no sign that Jeff lived there. As he finished his drink he heard the buzzer at the front door.

"Hello," Jeff said.

"Oi, oi, saveloy!" Jeff recognized Colin's standard greeting.

"I'm coming down," Jeff said. He had to unlock the parking garage and Brody waited at the entrance. Jeff climbed in and squeezed Colin over to the middle seat.

"Change of plans, boys. Let's go for a little ride first," Jeff said. He directed Brody to the clinic where Jessica worked.

"What the actual fuck are we doing here, Jeffy?" Brody said. Jeff told them to wait for him outside the entrance. He walked in and saw a woman at the front desk typing away at the computer.

"Hi, how can I help?" she said and smiled at Jeff.

"Actually, I'm looking for Jessica. Is she on break?" Jeff said he looked around. The woman looked confused.

"She's not working tonight, sir," she said with a concerned tone. Jeff realized he must have come off as a weird stalker.

"Oh, I'm her boyfriend, Jeff," he said. She relaxed her demeanour.

"Oh, Jeff. I've heard about you," she said. "Jess was here earlier to drop off some papers but she left. She said she was going for coffee and a movie. She was all dolled up." She looked at Jeff like he was a child who forgot to do his chores. "Did you forget to meet her?"

"Yeah, I guess so," Jeff laughed. "Miscommunication. Thanks," he said and he headed back outside. His heart raced as he got in the truck.

"Well," Brody said, "what the fuck?"

"Where's Jess? Colin said. Jeff didn't respond for a moment. His mind was being pulled in thousand directions.

"She's not here."

"I thought she was working tonight," Colin said.

"She's not."

"Then why the fuck did we drive all the way out here?" Brody said.

"I need a coffee," Jeff said. He looked straight ahead.

"Yeah. Shit. Why not? Let's get some damn coffee," Brody said and drove away. "You gonna let us know what the hell is going on?" Jeff kept his gaze fixed through the window.

"Just do me a favour, man. I'll explain after." They drove to the nearest coffee shop that had a patio. Jeff knew that Jess always liked to have a coffee on a café patio before a movie. They pulled up beside the shop and Jeff told Brody to stop.

"OK, you gonna tell me what this is all about, dick face?" Brody said. Jeff didn't answer but he pointed his chin to a couple at a small table. They were about to leave and she put her arm around him. He touched her face with the back of his hand and ran a finger up the spine of her black cocktail dress with the other hand as they kissed. It seemed to Jeff like it lasted forever. He felt like it would never end and he would just have to sit there and watch the disgusting display for the rest of time until Brody's voice caught his ear.

"Son of a bitch!" he said. "Let's go fuck this guy up." Jeff stopped him before he hopped out.

"No," Jeff said and he reached across Colin to grab Brody's arm. He hated confrontation and had always shied away rather than deal with an uncomfortable situation. This was about as uncomfortable as anything. He didn't like the possibility of trading blows with someone he wasn't certain he take on. If it did come to that, he knew Brody would join in. It was a recipe for disaster.

"Just take me home, man," Jeff said. They drove in silence. No music. No words were spoken. Just the sound of the truck and the road. Jeff went up to the apartment and packed his few belongings in garbage bags and backpacks while Colin and Brody waited in the truck. He was in the bathroom when the front door opened.

"Hello?" It was Jessica. "What's with all the trash?" Jeff came out of the bathroom and slung a bag over his shoulder.

"Trash. That's just the word I was thinking," he said.

"What are you talking about? What are you doing?"

"Getting rid of some trash." He put his bag down at the door with the rest of his things. He stopped and looked at her. "A little overdressed for work, aren't you?"

"Oh yeah," she said. "I went out for a drink with the girls." Jeff grabbed his Landon College mug from the cupboard and poured a drink. "Why are you acting so weird, Jeff?" He swallowed the drink in one shot and slammed the mug down.

"Why am I acting so weird? It's complicated. I guess it has a lot to do with that guy you were making out with at the café," he said. Jessica opened her mouth but no words came out. Jeff watched her eyes dart around as though the words she was looking for were written on the ceiling or cupboards. He saved her the trouble of spinning another lie and continued.

"I saw you with my own eyes, Jess. Don't feed me bullshit." They stared at each other for a few seconds. Jeff was mentally exhausted from the whole messy night. He exhaled and rinsed his mug. Jessica broke her silence.

"I didn't mean for this to happen, Jeff," she said. Jeff shook his head in disbelief.

"It was an accident, then?" he said.

"It's not what you think," she said. "Were you following me?" There was accusation in her voice.

"Don't make this about me. I'm not the one whoring around with some yuppie slime bag." Jeff dried the mug and put it in his bag. "I'm leaving," he said.

"You can't just leave me," she said.

"Turns out I can."

"What about the lease, huh?"

"Paid up. Landlord says you can stay if you want. Just sign a new lease by yourself."

"You piece of shit! You can't do this to me!"

"You did this to yourself," he said. "Maybe you can stay with Mr. Yuppie."

"Fine, Jeff. He's better than you anyway. Better job, better house, better lover. You come home late all the time after drinking and pay no attention to me. You know, we did it in his car right after you saw us."

"Oh, that's classy," Jeff said.

"Just leave, Jeff. I don't know why I even stayed with you. You're just a lowlife and a loser. Always will be," she said as she flipped her hair over her shoulder. "Probably runs in the family. Your kids will be losers. Bet your dad was, too.

Just like you. Can't fight genetics, Jeff." He spun around, hand raised, poised to bring it down across her face but something froze him in place. It wasn't a lingering love or a hope that, somehow, they could get past this nasty business and work things out. He stopped because he didn't want her to be right. Jessica didn't know about his dad and the things he did. He knew she was just trying to get under his skin but if he hit her, she would have been right without even knowing it. He slowly brought his hand down to his side. She hadn't flinched or cowered but her eyes were wide with fear. Jeff put on his backpack and opened the door.

"Coward," she said as he picked up his bags. He took one in each hand and walked to the elevator. Jessica stood in the doorway and shouted at him. "Go ahead, Jeff. Run away. You're not even a man," she said. The neighbours peeked their heads out to catch a glimpse of the commotion. "Don't even think about coming back, Jeff." The elevator door opened and Jeff put his bags inside. He looked at Jessica one last time before he raised his hand and then his middle finger. She slammed the door and he rode the elevator down. Brody leaned on his truck as he smoked a cigarette with Colin and they helped Jeff load his things.

"You good?" Brody said as they drove away.

"Yeah. I'm good," Jeff said. He stayed at

Brody's place that night and when he woke up there was coffee brewing.

"Want some?" Brody said. Jeff nodded and went to his backpack to get his favourite mug.

"So did Jess come clean last night or what?" Brody said.

"Yep."

"Crazy. I called her a slut bag on her way in. She probably had no idea what I was talking about," Brody said. Jeff laughed even though the situation was a nightmare. As bad as things were, he knew he made the right choice and his friends were there for him, in their own messed up kind of way.

"So what's the plan?" Brody said. Jeff shrugged his shoulders.

"Find a new place and start living life," he said.

"Sounds like a plan," Brody said. "Cool mug.

CHAPTER TEN
Slugger

Today

Jeff found an old newspaper clipping in the shoebox. It was stiff and yellowed by the years. It was a short article about the basketball team at Jeff's high school. Jeff smiled when he read the headline.

EAGLES SOAR OVER MUSTANGS IN JUNIOR B-BALL

The article was underlined where it mentioned Jeff and Brody. It was from their first game.

19 years ago

Jeff had just turned fifteen that week. His mom agreed to let him have some friends over on the weekend for a birthday party. She was more agreeable those days. She had started seeing a man named Keith. He was divorced but didn't have kids of his own. He reminded Jeff of all those cliché step-dad types on TV, right down to the collared shirt and sweater combination. Deb seemed to like to spend time with him so Jeff didn't give him a hard time. It didn't hurt that Jeff pretty much got to do whatever he wanted when Keith was around. Deb was so focused on her new man and Keith just tried to act like Jeff's best friend. Straight out of the cliché step-dad handbook. Keith had been coming around for a few months before Jeff's birthday. Maybe six or seven. Jeff couldn't remember exactly when.

Before the party, if you could call it that, Keith and Deb showed Jeff his present. They had set up an old TV in the finished part of the basement. The shiny new video game system was perched on a small cabinet next to it. Jeff didn't think it was real at first glance. He flicked the power on and turned around with what had to be the widest grin the world had ever seen.

"I'm not sure if he likes it," Keith said to Deb.

"No, I do," Jeff said before he clued in to Keith's joke.

"We knew you wanted it and Keith had an old

TV so happy birthday, sweetie," Deb said as she hugged him.

"Once you crazy kids break that thing in you'll have to show me how it's done," Keith said as he held up an imaginary game controller and twiddled his thumbs.

"Sure thing," Jeff said. "Thanks, guys. It's awesome."

"Have fun, slugger," Keith said. Jeff had no idea why Keith called him that. The last time Jeff even saw a baseball bat was in tee ball. Keith was weird like that.

Jeff left to meet his friends and bring them over. While he walked, he thought about how nice Keith acted all the time and that, for some reason, it was all some kind of show. Get in good with the son and it's smooth sailing with mom. Maybe he was just a dorky divorcée, though. Either way, Jeff didn't want to spend his free time with him. He met Brody and Colin at the park; a halfway point between all of their houses. Colin watched Brody shoot some hoops and they spotted Jeff.

"Hey, fucker," Brody said after he wrangled his ball.

"Sup, guys?" Jeff said. Brody passed the ball to Jeff.

"I'm telling you, man," Brody said. "You gotta come with me to basketball tryouts. Chicks fucking love ball players." Jeff took a shot and figured if he was out of the house more, he would see Keith less. He didn't hate the guy. He just preferred to not subject himself to his lame dad schtick all the time. He shot another basket and made up his mind.

"Let's go," he said. "You'll never guess what I got."

They ate pizza for dinner and fired up the games. They drank pop and played a few rounds. At one point, Deb called them up for cake and ice cream. Keith tried to relate to Colin and quoted some old British comedy show. Jeff waved his hand and shook his head at Colin to excuse Keith's attempt at being cool.

They finished their dessert and returned to the basement for the night. It was late morning when they all woke up and, before they left, Brody pressed Jeff again about basketball tryouts.

"We'll see." Jeff said even though he already decided that he would go.

Jeff did the tryout with Brody and they had to wait a few days for Coach Myers to post the roster. Jeff had all but forgotten about it until Brody barreled down the hall after school had ended. He told Jeff that they both made the cut. Jeff couldn't help but think that anyone who knew the rules would have made the team. Small town and all. They had practice every other day and their games were Friday nights. After the first two practices it was obvious that Jeff and Brody were a cut above the rest. They always seemed to know where to find each other on the court. Coach Myers worked his strategies around the two of them.

Their first game was a blowout. The Mustangs could barely keep the ball long enough to make a few passes before Jeff or Brody stole it away. The whole team only missed a few shots by the end of the game. It was total domination. It wasn't a fluke, either. Their next three games went the same way. During practices, Coach Myers spent most of his time with Jeff and Brody. He also worked a lot with Eddie. He was the tallest one so he played centre. Eddie always spent extra time working with the coach after practice was over. Myers had the team do some drills and called the three of them aside. He held a ball under one arm and stroked his moustache with his fingers.

"You boys have potential," he said. "You follow my advice and you'll be bumped up to the senior team next year."

"You got it, Coach," Brody said. Jeff nodded in agreement. He was proud of himself. This was his thing. He was a basketball player and he was really good.

Over the next few weeks, they won every game and Coach Myers spent more and more time with Jeff. At home, Jeff was a ghost. If he wasn't at a game or practice, he was shooting hoops at the park with Brody. His grades took a bit of a slip but it wasn't enough to draw any attention from his mom. She was too focused on Keith to notice anyway. They had a tough game coming up so Jeff wanted to be in top form. Both teams were undefeated but Adams High had a history of great teams. Coach Myers told the guys that Armstrong never had a team this good in all his years and he wanted to prove that they were the real deal. The whole team was amped for this one.

The game went as they expected for this first half. It wasn't as lopsided as their other games but they were still on top. Jeff tried to get Eddie going but he was playing like crap. Just after the second half started, Brody went in to grab a rebound against the bigger defender. He slipped on the landing and the Adams player came down on Brody's leg. Even through the noise of the crowd, everyone on the court stopped when they heard the bone snap. They both went down in a heap but Brody screamed and held his shin. The paramedics wheeled him out and took him to the hospital. Coach Myers put Barry Smith on in Brody's place. Jeff struggled to focus and Barry didn't help the situation. He was always out of position and didn't create any space. They started to miss more often and they couldn't keep the ball. With their star duo separated, The

Eagles couldn't keep up and ended up with their first loss of the season. Jeff was upset with the result but he was more concerned about Brody. Deb had sent Keith to pick Jeff up from the game. He stood next to his car and waved at Jeff.

"How'd you do, slugger?" Keith said as they drove off.

"Lost."

"Too bad. Maybe next time." Keith put his hand on Jeff's thigh to console him. Jeff looked down and Keith's hand retreated.

"Keith, I need to go to the hospital," Jeff said.

"Why? Are you alright?"

"Brody broke his leg. Real bad."

"Maybe we should check with your mom."

"Come on, man," Jeff said. Keith clenched his lips together in contemplation and agreed. Jeff visited with Brody for about twenty minutes even though he was still doped up from the pain medication. He signed Brody's cast before he left.

The next practice was more like a team meeting. Coach Myers told them that Brody was out. Probably for the rest of the season. Jeff looked around at his team. Eddie looked like hell. He had dark bags under his eyes and his skin was pale. More pale than usual. He looked like he hadn't slept in days. Myers went over the faults of the game they lost and sent the team out for scrimmage. They finished up and everyone was about to leave when Coach Myers called out from his office.

"Leetch, hang back a minute," he said. Jeff hurried across the gym and stopped outside the door.

"What's up, Coach?" Jeff said.

"Come on in. Let's talk." Jeff stepped in and Myers gave a casual gesture to the empty chair. "Shut the door," he said.

* * *

Eddie didn't show up for their next practice. Jeff hadn't seen him around school and figured he was sick. They started off with a quick scrimmage and then some drills. That's when all hell broke loose. The gym doors burst open and four police officers marched with purpose toward Coach Myers. The principal followed them and Jeff saw Eddie with his parents at the entrance just outside the gym doors. He looked even worse than before. His eyes were red and swollen. Eddie's mom had her arm around him and, even though he towered over her, he looked like a small child. The cops put Myers in handcuffs and led him away. There were so many voices that echoed in the gymnasium that Jeff couldn't hear what they said to him. The principal, Mrs. Saunders, gathered the team by the bleachers, told them that practices were cancelled until further notice and sent them home.

The next day at school, Jeff was pulled out of class and taken to the principal's office. His mom was there with a guidance counsellor and a policewoman.

"What's going on?" Jeff said. He sat in the empty seat and Mrs. Saunders explained the commotion at practice the day before. Coach Myers had been arrested for sexual assault. Eventually, he confessed it to the police. They were interviewing the whole team to try and get all the facts straight. They asked Jeff about his interactions with Myers and what they would talk about. They wanted to know if he noticed any odd or inappropriate behaviour. As Jeff answered, the officer wrote in her little notepad. They questioned him about the other guys on the team, if Myers showed any extra attention to anybody in particular and if anything happened after the games or practices. They asked and asked and asked. It seemed like it went on for hours. Jeff's head started to hurt when the officer said she had one last question.

"Jeff, I know this is a lot and you've been very helpful but I have to ask you this. Did he make any advances, touch you or make you do anything sexual in nature?" Jeff looked at each person in the room before he answered. Deb's face was drained of any colour and tears welled in her eyes. Jeff looked the officer dead in the eyes and lied.

"No," he said. "Never." Deb rubbed his back and sighed in obvious relief. Mrs. Saunders asked Jeff to keep their conversation private while they finished their interviews with everyone. She told him to take the rest of the day off to clear his head. Jeff and his mom got up to leave but Saunders had something to add.

"I almost forgot," she said. "We found a temporary coach so practice is still on for tomorrow." Jeff nodded and left with his mom. In the car, she glanced over to him every few seconds.

"Do you want talk about all this?" Deb said.

"Nothing to talk about," Jeff said. His head was still sore from the interrogation. Deb made some soup when they got home. Jeff ate in silence and when he finished he told her he was off to visit Brody.

"I'll be back before dinner," he said and stopped at the door. "Do me a favour?"

"What's that, honey?"

"Don't tell Keith about all this. He'll just act all weird."

"Sure, sweetie. Whatever you want."

Brody's mom answered the door when he got there. Jeff could tell that she wanted to ask him about what happened but the words wouldn't come out.

"Hey, Jeff," she said. Her mouth was still half open but she stopped herself. "Hey," she said again.

"Hey. Is Brody upstairs?" Jeff said.

"Oh yeah, Tommy's in his room," she said. "Head on up, hun."

"Thanks," Jeff said. He knocked on Brody's door as he walked in.

"Oh hey, fucker!" Brody said.

"Hey Tommy." Jeff mimicked Brody's mom.

"Asshole. Wait," Brody looked at his watch, "you cutting class?"

"Nope. Saunders gave me the afternoon off. Got interviewed by the cops about Myers."

"Oh yeah, they were here earlier," Brody said. "My mom is freaking out."

"Yeah I noticed," Jeff said.

"What a perv. At least they caught him before he got anyone else. Pretty shitty for Eddie, though."

"For sure," Jeff said. He wanted to get off of the subject. "Anyway, what's up with you?"

"Bored as fuck," Brody said. They chatted for a bit, watched some TV, and Jeff headed out. While he walked home, he thought about Eddie. He had looked completely broken and exhausted but Jeff knew he was courageous and strong. Jeff knew it because he felt the exact opposite. He was afraid and ashamed of what people would say. What they would think if he admitted what Eddie had the courage to admit. Jeff knew they would believe him but he didn't want to believe it himself. He remembered something he heard Eddie's mom say as they dragged Myers away.

"He won't hurt anybody again." It was something he had heard a hundred times before on TV shows and movies after the good guys caught the bad guy. But the words were hollow. They were just something to say. He already hurt somebody and nothing could ever change that. Jeff didn't tell anyone what happened. He figured it wouldn't do any good. They already caught Myers and Jeff didn't want any pity or attention. Especially that kind of attention. He hoped it would just go away like a bad nightmare that forget about over time.

Today

A tear fell from Jeff's eye and landed on the aged newspaper. He wiped his eyes and crumpled the article in his hand. He slammed his fist on the small table and the contents of the shoebox scattered out on the table and floor. He finished his drink and got up to make another. After all these years, he knew one thing for sure. Some nightmares just won't die, no matter how much you try to drown them.

CHAPTER ELEVEN
Thick As Thieves

Jeff shoved the keepsakes back in the box and took it out to the living room. He dropped it on the coffee table and leaned back in the recliner. He needed a break from the memory box so he smoked a cigarette and stared at the ceiling. His eyes were sore and his head pounded so he went out the side door. The fresh air felt good so he lit a smoke and checked out the backyard. There was a rusted old swingset at the back fence. Jeff walked across the grass and pushed the hard plastic seat of the swing with his foot. It squeaked back and forth from years of neglect. He smiled as the swing slowed to a stop. He ran his hand along the monkey bars and leaned against the rail. It was all brown now but it used to be a bright metallic blue and shiny white.

29 years ago

Jeff got home from school just as his dad pulled in the driveway.

"Hey, boy-o!" Jimmy said as he jerked the car to a halt. "Wait until you see what I got." Jimmy loosened the bungee cords that held the trunk closed. All Jeff could see was brown cardboard. It was big and long but he had no idea what it was. Jimmy slid the box out and there were big bold letters on the side. Deluxe Swingset.

"Pretty sweet, huh?"

"Oh yeah!" Jeff bounced up and down with excitement. Jimmy put the box in the backyard.

"Whatcha say we put this baby together after dinner?" Jimmy said.

"Yay!"

"Come on, boy-o," Jimmy said as he tousled Jeff's hair and led him inside. Deb was in the kitchen making dinner. Potato soup by the look of it. The big pot was on the stove and steam forced its way through the edges of the lid. Jeff did his homework while he waited for dinner. After they ate, Jimmy went to the basement and came up with his old green toolbox. Jeff followed him around like a shadow. He was excited to help his dad and even more excited to test out the new swingset. Jimmy opened the box and laid out all of the pieces. He handed Jeff the instructions.

"You're in charge of the tools, too, boy-o," he said. Jeff nodded. They had it halfway done when Deb came outside with some drinks for them.

"Here's a little something for my construction crew," she said. Jimmy took a sip.

"Whew! That's some strong lemonade," he said. Jeff drank some and imitated his dad.

"Ahh."

"You big strong men be careful," Deb said and she sat in a lawn chair, sipped her drink and watched them assemble the new addition to the backyard. Every now and then she got up and brought refills. Jimmy hammered a post into the ground and looked at Jeff.

"You should give it a go," he said. Jeff smiled wide.

"Really?"

"Yeah, why not?" Jimmy flipped the handle of the hammer toward Jeff.

"Wow," Jeff said. Jimmy guided Jeff and told him to start slow.

"Once you get going, give it some gusto," he said. Jeff tapped a few hits and then took bigger swings. "Easy now," Jimmy said. And just as the words came out, Jeff slammed the hammer down on his thumb and yelped with pain and surprise. "Oops. Medic!" Jimmy yelled toward the house. Deb came out and jogged over to Jeff. He held his thumb and when he saw his mom he couldn't help but let the tears out.

"Oh dear," Deb said. "Come with me, Jeffy." She took him inside and made him hold his hand under the cold water in the kitchen sink.

Jeff wiped his nose with his sleeve as Deb turned off the tap. She took him to the kitchen table to examine the injury.

"Looks like this'll be fine," she said. "Let's get you a bandage, just in case."

After they finished in the house, she sent him back outside. When Jeff rounded the corner, his dad swung the hammer one last time and took a step back to survey his work. Jeff stopped to watch him and marvelled at the beauty of it, too. It was so new and different. It changed the whole backyard. It was just a swingset but it was in his yard and he could use it whenever he wanted to. The late afternoon sun gleamed off the bright blue beams and white accents. Jeff was in his own world and hadn't noticed his dad looking at him.

"Whatcha think, boy-o?"

"It's awesome."

"You haven't even tried it yet," Jimmy said as he swooped both arms toward the swing to invite Jeff over. Jeff ran across the yard and jumped on the swing. Jimmy played around and hung himself by the legs from the monkey bars.

"Get your big butt offa there, Leetch," Deb yelled. She held another lemonade up in the air and Jimmy joined her on the patio. They sat and watched while Jeff played. He stayed on there for hours. He went back and forth from the swing to the bars to the slide. It was fantastic.

He would have kept going but as the sun went down and the mosquitoes started to bite, Jeff's parents called him in for the night. He was still a ball of energy when his mom told him to get ready for bed. He got changed, laid down, and Deb came in to say goodnight.

"Did you have a good day, Jeffy," she said. Jeff nodded and smiled. "Did you thank your dad?" Jeff made a thoughtful face and realized that he hadn't so he hopped off of the bed and ran out to the living room.

"Thanks, dad," he said. Jimmy smiled at him and Jeff scampered back to his room. Deb read him a story and he dozed off a few pages in.

Today

Jeff stared at the rusted old thing. It looked like a strong wind could blow it over but he saw it how it used to be. He was about to go back inside when he heard a voice from the yard next door. It was Mary.

"Jeff," she said, "how's it going over there?" He turned and smiled at her.

"Pretty good." He looked at the swingset. "Just taking a little break."

"Understandable," Mary said. She looked down with sadness on her face. "Always so sad when this disease claims another life."

"The liver—" Jeff stopped himself when he

couldn't remember the exact name of it.

"No, the drink. Got my Fred, too." She looked away toward nothing when she said his name. "A long time ago."

"Oh, I'm sorry to hear that."

"Well," she said as she took in a breath, "life goes on." Jeff sensed that she didn't want to talk about it so he changed the subject.

"I never did ask before. How long did you know my mom?" Mary smiled.

"Ever since I moved in here ten years ago. She brought over some coffee cake after the moving truck left. She said I deserved a snack after such a hard day." Jeff nodded in recognition. His mom always used food to comfort. "We sat and talked for a while. After that, we were just thick as thieves." Mary giggled a bit although Jeff could tell that it was laced with grief. He had assumed that she was just a helpful neighbour but he realized that she probably knew his mom better than he did. Mary had held herself together well considering she just lost such a close friend.

"I was all alone after Fred passed and she'd been on her own for a while there with Keith leaving and all." She looked off to the distance again.

"Can I ask you something about her?" Jeff said.

"What's that?"

"Well, I found an old shoebox with some AA chips in it but there's a bunch of liquor in the house."

"Yes," she said, "your mom was trying to stop for a bit there."

"When?"

"A few years back," Mary said. "She did well there for a stretch. I guess after she found out that your dad died she took a turn for the worse."

"What did you say?"

CHAPTER TWELVE
Relapse

"Oh dear," Mary said, "you didn't know."

"When? How?" Jeff said.

"Why don't you come inside?" she said. "I'll make some tea." She waited for him in her driveway and let him in. Jeff sat in an armchair while Mary was in the kitchen. She popped her head around the corner.

"Sugar?"

"No, thank you," Jeff said. Mary came out with a teapot and cups on a serving tray. She poured them both a cup and took a sip. Jeff just sat and waited. She put her cup down and took a deep breath.

"Oh goodness," she said. "Where to begin?"

"Tell me about the AA chips," Jeff said as he picked his tea. Mary shifted in her seat like she was about to go for a long drive.

"Well it was about a year after I moved in. She was always so lonely. Even when we would get together, I could sense it in her. She usually just stayed home in the evenings. During they day she worked as a receptionist at that insurance place downtown. She would usually only drink at home. She had nothing else to do, really. Eventually, she started indulging at lunch hour and break times. Things got worse and it started affecting her work. They ended up firing her because she just wasn't up to snuff. I came over one day to play cards and I could see her through the front door, passed out on the couch. She didn't even hear me knocking. There were cigarette burns on the rug and the coffee table. The place was a mess. After seeing what happened to my Fred, I sobered her up and brought her to some meetings.

"We went together the first few times but she was doing so well and she just ran with it. She never liked the religious parts of it all but Deb always said 'Mary, if it works, it works.' Oh, every now and then she would slip up and have a drink but nothing she didn't bounce back from. Just a few bumps in the road. She was always so happy to show off her chips when she got them. She tried to play it cool, you know, leaving it on the table when we played cards but I knew she was proud of herself." Mary paused with a catch in her throat and sipped some tea. Jeff nodded along as she spoke and held his tea but didn't drink it. She looked at Jeff with such sorrow in her eyes before she went on.

"She was almost a year clean, I think. I never saw the one year coin if she got one. It's hard to say. She had to start over a few times in the beginning. Anyway, she came over for tea one Sunday and saw the newspaper on the table. I thought she was just having a casual look at an article but when I came out of the kitchen, her face was completely drained of colour. She didn't even respond to me when I asked her what was wrong. She just stood up and mumbled something about having to leave. I watched her go back to her house and figured she needed some time to herself so I let her be. After I cleaned up, I had a look at the newspaper. As I read it, I realized what shook her up so bad. There was a bad car crash. Drunk driver hit a hydro pole. There was a picture of the car all smashed up. It said Jimmy Leetch and his ten year old son were both pronounced dead at the scene."

"Son?" Jeff didn't ask so much as say it out loud to try and process it. Jeff couldn't believe his ears. He just found out that he had a brother and he died all in the same breath. His father died and his mom didn't tell him. "No," Jeff said, "there has to be some mistake." Mary clasped her hands together on her lap and shook her head.

"I'm afraid it's true, dear. Later that night, I went to check on Deb and she was in shambles. Drinking right out of a big bottle, listening to sad songs on full blast and crying her eyes out. I tried to make her give me the bottle but she wouldn't. My heart just broke for her. All that hard work getting sober was wasted. Sure, she slipped before but it was just a cocktail here and there. Nothing like this."

"But it had been forever. She hated him."

"That wasn't it. I'm sure that was part of it but, no. After everything she told me about him I was wondering why it shook her so bad, too. When I asked her about it she just cried more. I stayed with her that night. She ran out of booze pretty fast and I put her to bed. The next morning, I was cooking some breakfast when she came in the kitchen and sat at that little white table. She didn't say good morning or anything. She just started pouring her heart out. You see, she didn't know that your dad remarried and had another child. All those years of loneliness and heartache tore her up. His death shocked her, of course, but she was devastated that he had made this new life for himself and she wasn't good enough for him to stick around. What made him stay with this new family? How could he walk out on you guys so easily? What was so unbearable about her to warrant abandonment? All the men in her life abandoned her. Her own dad, Jimmy, and then Keith. Even y—" Mary stopped herself before she finished but Jeff knew what she was about to say. "Sorry, dear. It's not my place." Jeff shook his head to forgive her.

"It's alright," he said and Mary went on.

"She was in such a state. Wallowing in self pity. She took some time off from work and even went to the funeral. I begged her not to. No good could come from it but she had already made up her mind. She came back from it worse than she started. Can't blame her. It must have been an awful thing to see a child laid to rest. She never got over the whole thing and there wasn't anything I could do to help her. She tried to quit every now and again but it never lasted long. Her body just couldn't take it anymore." Mary wiped away a tear. Jeff sunk back in the chair with the weight of the revelations. He realized that his hand had moved to the pocket of his jacket and he circled the edges of the flask with his fingers. He sat there for a moment in silence and felt the metal. He ran the tips of his fingers over the grooves of the engraved inscription. Mary broke the silence.

"I know this is a lot to throw on you, today especially. And you've still got so much to do," she said as she stood up. She took a pen and small notepad from the side table to jot something down. She tore off a sheet and handed it to Jeff. "Here's my number," she said. "Just hang on to it. If you want to talk, I'm usually always here."

"Sure," Jeff said. He put the paper in his pocket and stood up. He turned to the door and, as if he were in a trance, walked out. Mary followed him to the door and saw him out. She stood on the small porch while he walked back to his mother's house. Before he went back in, he turned to Mary.

"Thanks for the tea," he said. She smiled and he went back in. His feet took him straight to the kitchen and he grabbed the half empty bottle on the counter. This time, he didn't bother mixing a drink. He took the bottle to the couch. He sat down and took the flask out his jacket pocket. He held it in his palms and stared at the initials carved in the metal. He slowly unscrewed the cap and thought of his dad. He pressed the opening to his lips and drew his head back. He didn't stop until every drop was gone. He stared around the small house and every minute or so he took a big drink from the bottle until it was nearly empty. His mind slowed, his eyes grew heavy and he laid his head on the arm of the couch.

CHAPTER THIRTEEN
Heirloom

Jeff woke up about an hour later. He used the bathroom and got a bottle of water from the fridge. He wandered around the house and peered in the rooms with no real purpose. He went to the basement, emptied a box of magazines and started to gather some of the things that he could use at home. Laundry soap, canned food, and some other household stuff. He figured he could save himself a trip to the grocery store. His head was still tight and sore. He felt a bit dizzy, too. He stopped rummaging to grab some aspirin and another water from the kitchen. He took a drink and looked at the shoebox on the table when the light sparkled off the metallic finish of the sobriety medallions. He took the box in one hand and shook the contents to scramble them up. Jeff looked at all the little mementoes and papers with disdain. He had no idea why she kept all these things. Just a bunch of useless junk. All he saw was a casket for the pain and demons of yesterday.

He was about to toss in the trash can but he stopped himself. He couldn't do it. He took it downstairs and put it in the box he had packed. He brought everything up and grabbed some food from the cupboards. He opened the freezer and stared at the big bottles of vodka. They seemed to stare back at him. They practically called to him. He put them in the box and his phone vibrated in his pocket. He pulled it out and answered.

"Yeah?"

"Jeff, it's Colin. Look, I'm sorry for calling today but something's happened." His voice was panicked.

"No. It's OK," Jeff said. "What's up, man?"

"It's Brody..."

"What about him?" Jeff said as he tapped the box with his foot.

"Christ. I... I can't even believe it."

"What, Colin?"

"The other night at the pub, he drove home and there was an accident..." Colin paused for a moment and Jeff's stomach turned as if he knew what Colin was about to say. "He's dead, Jeff." Colin burst into tears. "My God. He's dead." Jeff didn't respond. His hands shook and his head started to spin. His phone slid from his fingers and dropped to the floor. Jeff fell to his hands and knees. His stomach rotted and churned. He pulled himself up on the trash can and threw up in it. He could still hear Colin on the phone. He picked it up off the floor and cleared his throat.

"Jeff, say something, for God's sake," Colin said through tears.

"I... I need to go," Jeff said. "Call you later." He hung up before Colin said anything else. Jeff stood in the kitchen and didn't move. All of the things that Jeff and Brody did together flashed before his eyes while he stood there. He felt numb and stuck in place. Jeff stared down at the box next to his feet. The bright red bottle caps stood out like beacons. A tear dropped on one of them and rolled down the bottleneck. He didn't realize that he was crying.

Eventually, he made his way to the couch. He sat down and wiped the tears from his cheeks. He decided to have one last smoke before he left. He was sitting in the same spot that his dad used to sit in night after night. It was the same spot where his mom had fallen asleep with a cigarette and left burn marks in the old carpet. As he butted out his smoke, he heard their voices in his head. He felt their movements pulse through the house. All the laughter and arguments. The good times and the bad. Their familiar, everyday routines echoed in the creaks and cracks of the houses bones as they settled. He was in the same spot now because, despite all his carefully placed resentments, he was just like them. He had spent most of his life trying to convince himself otherwise but it was impossible to deny. He rubbed his eyes and cracked his neck. It was time to go.

Jeff walked through the house again in slow, exhausted steps. The floorboards groaned under his feet in the exact spots they always had. He soaked in the sounds and flashes of memories. He turned off the lights and closed the doors as he went.

He stopped in the kitchen and looked at the box he had packed. He knelt down to lift it but stopped. He picked up one of the bottles and held it out in front of himself. He jerked his hand as if to test the weight of it and put it down. His eyes moved to the shoebox and back to the bottle. He was still holding it. He let his fingers slide off of it and he picked up the shoebox.

* * *

Jeff walked across the lawn to Mary's doorstep. He looked back at his old house one more time before he knocked. Mary opened the door and smiled. Jeff could tell that she had been crying.

"Oh, Jeff," Mary said and she looked at the box. "Everything all right, dear?"

"I just wanted to say thank you again for everything you did today." Mary relaxed her posture.

"Not at all, dear." She nodded toward the box. "What's all that?"

"Oh right," Jeff said. "You knew my mom best. These things were important to her and I think she would have wanted you to have them." Jeff handed the shoebox to Mary. She opened it and smiled.

"Isn't that sweet of you," she said as she picked up the gold coin. "Oh look. She did make it to one year." Mary looked over to Deb's house. "You must have a lot of boxes over there. Do you need a ride?" Jeff looked at the house and smiled.

"No thanks," he said. "I got everything I needed." Mary looked a little confused. "There is one more thing."

"What's that, dear?" Mary said.

"I was hoping you could take this." Jeff reached inside his jacket and handed her the flask. She took it and ran her palm over the initials.

"JL. Jeff Leetch?"

"No," Jeff said. "Jimmy Leetch." Mary moved it back toward him.

"Are you sure you don't want to keep this? I mean, in light of everything we talked about?" she said.

"I'm sure," Jeff said as he walked down the stairs. "I won't need it anymore."

* * *

Jeff went home and laid in bed. The sun crept over the tall buildings of downtown and woke him. He called work and took a few days off. They gave him as much time as he needed after he told them what happened. He touched base with Colin and they talked to each other almost every night for hours. Jeff had to keep himself busy while he waited for Brody's funeral or he was certain he would go crazy. He cleaned his apartment, threw out all the old pizza boxes and bought actual groceries. He spent his afternoons in the park and read. On his way home he would pass the community centre and look at the events posted.

The funeral was at the same cemetery as his mom's. When Jeff got there, he sat next to Colin. He was with his parents and they saved Jeff a seat. A minister walked toward the gathering. *Unbelievable*, Jeff thought. It was the same minister who spoke at his mom's service. He raised his hands to call attention and everyone straightened up in their seats. As the minster spoke, Jeff could have said the words along with him. The minister finished and, as the casket was lowered, Jeff started to cry. He realized that his tears were not just for his friend. He never properly mourned his mother or his father. Even the half brother he had never met. Jeff let it all out in that moment. Everyone there cried for his friend but on the inside, Jeff was at four funerals all at once. He said goodbye to all of them during the moment of silence.

After the service, Jeff stood up and hugged Colin.

"Call me later?" Jeff said.

"Sure thing, mate." Jeff left and hoped that he would only ever return to that cemetery to visit his mom and Brody.

He spent the afternoon on his usual park bench and stopped at the community centre on his way home. Something caught his eye on the schedule and he went inside to check it out. There was a man at a podium and a small audience. Jeff stayed in the doorway while the man spoke. He was certain that he had seen him before but could not remember where. The man saw Jeff and stopped. The audience turned around in their chairs for a moment before the skinny old man went on. He finished a few minutes later and told everyone to help themselves to some coffee. He shook a womans hand and walked toward Jeff. As he came closer,

Jeff locked on to his bugged out eyes and remembered where he knew him from.

"Jeff, isn't it?" he said and offered his hand.

"Yeah. Good to see you again Mr.—"

"Frank," he interrupted. "Only first names here."

"Right," Jeff said and shook his hand. He looked around the room. "So you're not at, what was it, Greenstone anymore?"

"Oh I just do this a few nights a week," Frank said. "Would you like to stay for the last half?" Jeff looked around the room and nodded.

"Absolutely," he said.

"That's great," Frank said and smiled. He showed Jeff to an empty seat and returned to the podium. Everyone sat at their chairs before he started again.

"Welcome back. Would anyone like to share?" he said as he looked around. Jeff raised his hand just enough to get Frank's attention.

"Yes, sir. Come on up." Jeff stood up and traded places with Frank. He looked down at his hands as he rubbed them together. He took a long, slow breath and looked up.

"My name is Jeff," he said, "and I'm an alcoholic."

THE END

About Brian Colborne

My name is Brian Colborne and I am a Canadian author and family man. I've worked in the wireless tech industry, the financial sector and telecom sales (those people that called you at home and tried to sell you stuff you didn't really need. Sorry about that). Scattered in there were stints as a bass player and songwriter in a Brit Rock band. I live with my amazing wife and two wonderful sons in London, Ontario. I grew up here, went to school here, and hope to stay here for the rest of my life.

If you enjoyed reading this book and would like to receive my newsletter for specials and updates on upcoming books, please visit www.bcolborne.com to sign up. Your email address will never be given out or sold to anyone and I will limit my newsletter to once every few weeks.

Stay Connected

Website: http://www.bcolborne.com
Twitter: @bcolborne
Facebook: facebook.com/BriColAuthor

www.ingramcontent.com/pod-product-compliance
Lightning Source LLC
Chambersburg PA
CBHW020824150626
46554CB00018B/1890